P9-AFZ-740

HERGÉ

★

THE ADVENTURES OF

TINTIN

★

THE CALCULUS AFFAIR

LITTLE, BROWN AND COMPANY
New York Boston

This edition first published in the UK in 2007
by Egmont UK Limited
Translated by Leslie Lonsdale-Cooper and Michael Turner

www.casterman.com
www.tintin.com
Little, Brown Books for Young Readers is a division of Hachette Book Group, Inc.
The Little, Brown name and logo are trademarks of Hachette Book Group, Inc.

Little, Brown Books for Young Readers
Hachette Book Group
1290 Avenue of the Americas, New York, NY 10104
Visit us at lb-kids.com

ISBN 978-0-316-35724-1
21
APS
Printed in China

L.10EIFN000665.C010

THE CALCULUS AFFAIR

So much for your peace and quiet, Captain! Look over there. There's a big storm brewing.
Yes, it's high time we got back to the house.
WOOOUIHHH
My hat! . . . Hey! . . . My hat!
Thundering typhoons! My very best hat!
BRROM
Ugh! Here comes the rain.
Good old Nestor! He's come to meet us with an umbrella.
Thank you, Nestor. We'd have been absolutely soaked.
By the whiskers of Kûrvi-Tasch! Someone else is watching them already.

Well, we're home again . . . and none too soon, either!
RRIIING
The telephone, Nestor.
Hello? . . . No Madam, I am not Mr Cutts the butcher! . . . No, Madam . . . NO, Madam! . . . Fiddle-de-dee, Madam!
. . . That's at least the twentieth time . . .
Quite so, Nestor. But one must always keep one's temper . . . especially with a lady . . . And besides, Nestor, you should never telephone during a storm: it is extremely dangerous.
That's that. And now, my friend, I think I'll just have a quiet drink, if you don't mind.
CRACK
Blistering barnacles! That flash of lightning wasn't far away.
In fact, I . . .
GLING
BLING
CLING
?
!
Look at that!
?
The funny thing is, that happened AFTER the clap of thunder.
RRING RRING
Hello? . . . What? . . . Lamb chops?! . . . No, Madam, I am not Mr Cutts the butcher! And what's more Madam, it is highly dangerous to telephone during a storm. You should know better! And the best of luck, Madam!
CRACK
BANG
?

Vanished! . . . Vaporized! . . . Poor Captain! How dreadful!
Billions of blistering barnacles!
If I ever lay hands on that female . . .
CRACK
DLING
CLING
BLING
?
CLING
BLING
CLING
Thundering typhoons! My priceless Chinese vase!
How in the world could that vase have broken? Anyway, it certainly wasn't done by the lightning.
I just can't make it out.
PLING
Again! . . .
WOOAH
SSSS
GRRR
GRRR
My beautiful Florentine mirror!
But this time I know the answer. Your confounded Snowy. This is his handiwork.
But look here, Captain, that's absurd . . . How could he possibly . . .
CRACK
Billions of bilious blue blistering barnacles! Now the electricity has gone! That's the last straw!
THUMP THUMP
THUMP
Ten thousand thundering typhoons! Now what's that?
THUMP
THUMP
THUMP

What shall I do, sir? Shall I . . . Shall I open it?
Yes, Nestor.
Ah! At last!
Hey! You there . . . Who d'you think you are?
Billions of blue blistering barnacles! That's a fine way to introduce yourself. And what d'you want here, anyway?
That's a long story, old boy . . .
Ah, the lights!
Yes, quite a story . . . I was driving along when, crack! . . . my windscreen shattered, and all the other windows as well. In that downpour too! So I said to myself: "Jolyon," (that's my name), Jolyon Wagg, of the Rock Bottom Insurance . . .
How nice! . . .
"Jolyon," I said to myself, "what are you going to do now? " . . . Then I saw your house. "I'll shelter there," I said . . . Here, take my coat, old chap.
You'd better stay here till the rain stops.
Nice little place you've got here. Must say I prefer something more modern, but still . . .
Oho! had a tiff with the wife, eh?
I . . . it was probably the lightning.
Lightning? . . . Ha! ha! ha! And I'll bet you weren't insured, eh, you old rascal? Well what a bit of luck that Jolyon Wagg dropped in: he'll soon fix you up with a neat little policy.
How kind.
Is that whisky you're drinking? You can pour one for me while you're about it. Not that I like the stuff: I'm just thirsty, that's all.
Not bad armchairs, these. I don't stand on ceremony, you know. A bit of a clown, that's me. Never a dull moment with me around, you bet!
I take after my Uncle Anatole; he was a barber, you know. Oh, you should have met him! A proper caution, he was. Always telling stories, make you die of laughing . . . Like this one . . . There were two men in a railway carriage, see . . .
Cheers!
!
?
?
CLING

Did . . . did you see that? . . . I was just standing, my glass in my hand, and . . .
Oho! that's fun!
You think that's funny, eh? Is that all you've got to say?
If you could have seen yourself when that glass blew up! Your face was a scream!
Ha! ha! ha! Reminds me of that story of Uncle Anatole's . . . Half a mo' while I think of it . . . Oh yes. There was this man went into a pub, see, and ordered a pint of beer. He was just going to drink it, when . . .
!
!
?
CLING
Blow me! Did . . . did you see that? . . . Just like yours! . . . I don't get it!
I think it's fun!
I . . . er . . . think the storm has passed. I must be on my way.
I've wasted quite enough time here, anyway. Goodbye!
By the way . . . er . . . what about your insurance against lightning?
No thank you, Mr Wagg. I'm insured against everything under the sun.
Yes, everything. My life's insured against accident; against hailstones, rain, floods, tidal waves and tornadoes; against cholera, 'flu, and colds in the head; moths, weevils and grasshoppers . . . The whole lot! In fact, sir, the only things I'm not insured against are insurance agents!
You old humbug, you! Well, that's all settled. I'll send you a policy . . . No, better still, I'll bring it myself. That'll give us a chance to have another chinwag together.
'Bye for now!
SLAM
He can go to the devil – him, and his insurance, and his Uncle Anatole!
Calm down, Captain. Shouldn't we try to solve the mystery of all this broken glass?
You're right. But still, I . . .
BANG
BANG
BANG
Listen! Shots!

They came from outside.
There's someone coming . . . Oh, it's Professor Calculus, on the way back from his laboratory.
Did you hear those shots?
No, it's over now. The rain has stopped.
Professor, just look at your hat! Excuse me . . .
Look! A bullet has gone right through it!
Oh! See! . . . a hole!
I can't understand it at all. The moths never used to make such big holes as these.
Quick, Captain. Let's have a look round the park.
Right. Just let me fetch a torch, and I'll be with you.
Calculus certainly came along this path . . .
Captain! Snowy's picked up a scent. Come on, let's follow him.
Oh! Look there!
Wooah!
Blistering barnacles! Do you think he's . . .
No: he's alive. His heart's beating . . . faintly . . .
We must send for the police at once.
You stay here while I go and telephone.
Blistering barnacles, what an evening! What an evening!
Oh, sir! . . . Sir! Something terrible's happened!
In heaven's name, what's the matter now?

Oh, sir! Your beautiful Venetian chandelier, upstairs. Smashed to smithereens, sir!
Later, Nestor, tell me later.
Hello? . . . Police station? . . . This is Marlinspike . . . What? You're Mr Cutts, the butcher?! Blistering barnacles! I . . . I beg your pardon. Wrong number.
I'm sure the number's 412 . . .
RRRING
RRRING
Hello? . . . What? No, Madam, I am not Mr Cutts the butcher! . . . No Madam! . . . No Madam! . . . Fiddle-de-dee, Madam!
SLAM
Marlinspike Police Station . . . Who is that? . . . Oh yes, Captain . . . Yes . . . Shots you say? Someone injured, in the grounds? Very good, Captain, we'll be with you right away.
. . . and another vase, sir . . .
Later, Nestor, later.
Oh, you've come back?
To fetch some water. The poor fellow wants a drink.
He talks with a strong foreign accent . . . He seems to be badly hurt.
Here we are. You'll soon see . . .
!
Great snakes! The wounded man . . . he's vanished!
I say . . . are you sure this is the place?
Absolutely certain. Look, the grass is flattened down!
WOOAH
WOOAH
WOOAH
OH!
!

Blistering barnacles! Come out of there, or I'll shoot!
Mercy! Have pity! Please don't kill me! I wouldn't harm a fly . . . I'm just a simple fellow . . .
Blistering barnacles, you don't have to tell me that! Just explain what you're doing down there!
Me? . . . I . . . I was hiding.
Somebody tried to murder me! I was walking towards my car . . . then suddenly: Bang! Bang! . . . So I said to myself, I said, "Jolyon, someone's trying to kill you . . ."
Wait . . . I can hear a car. It must be the police.
Are you the one who telephoned? . . . Good. The doctor and the ambulance are just behind us. Where is the casualty?
Here I am, Mr Inspector . . . Jolyon Wagg . . . That's me . . .
You've been shot?
Me? No.
But didn't you report that you'd found a wounded man?
Well, we did, but now he's vanished.
Then why were you pretending to be the victim?
But I am, Mr Inspector; I'm the victim of an attack; I was shot at. So I said to myself, "Jolyon," I said . . .
They weren't firing at him, sergeant, but the shots must have whistled past him. In fact one went through Calculus's hat.
And who, pray, is Calculus?
Calculus? He's a friend of mine. He came back to the hole with a house in his hat . . . No, I mean . . . Anyway, Tintin told me . . .
And who is Tintin?
Tintin? But this is Tintin! Here . . .
Hey, now where's he gone?
Go on, Snowy! Seek it out!

The wounded man got away through this hole in the hedge.
You've lost the scent, eh Snowy? I can guess why.
He was picked up by a car waiting here for him. There's nothing to be done. Come on, let's go back to the others.
. . . You mean the glass just broke by itself?
By itself, yes sergeant! And then . . .
Where have you sprung from?
Snowy picked up a scent. But it didn't lead anywhere.
There's nothing more we can do here. We'd better go back to the house; we can talk things over more easily there.
Yes, this case looks a hopeless muddle to me.
Next morning . . .
?
. . . TIN . . . BLOP . . . BLUB . . . PLOB

Blub . . . blub . . . blub . . .
Why? What's up, Captain?
There . . . in the . . . Blub . . .
Wait a minute. Rinse your mouth out first. I'll bring you a glass of water.
Hey, Snowy, be quiet. What are you howling for?
CLING
You . . . you . . . blub . . . you see! We're, we're bewitched, I tell you . . . We're bewitched!
And an hour later
Blistering barnacles, I don't know about you Tintin, but all this carry-on is beginning to get on my nerves.
Yes, ever since yesterday there's been a strange feeling about the house.
YOW-OW-OW . . . YOW-OW-OOOW . . .
?
?
ZZIING
Let's go and see. That sounded like a smash on the road.
?
!
MILCO
5431 P
I . . . I don't know how it happened. I was driving along as usual . . . Suddenly, just as I passed your gate, crash! bang! . . . There was a terrible noise . . . and look what happened . . . It's got me beat . . .
Well, what do you make of it? It's exactly what happened to that creature, Jolyon Wagg.
It's fantastic.
TSSI-I-I-I-I-I-I
Look out!

Road-hog! Steam-roller! . . . Bully! . . . Dipsomaniac! . . . Nitwit!
Thomson and Thompson!!
Yes, it's us. Hello . . . The local police have told us all about that business last night. So we're here to investigate.
To be precise: we're here.
At the right moment, too!
Just take a look here. This good fellow was driving quietly along past the front of the house when, CRACK . . . You see what happened? . . . What do you make of it?
MILCO
The whole thing began last night . . .
Why, here comes our friend Calculus.
Hello, Cuthbert. Are you going away?
No, no. I'm just going away.
I'm flying to Geneva, where I'm taking part in a congress on nuclear physics.
To Geneva? . . . But you never mentioned it to me before.
No, not for very long: only two or three days. I must go now; I've just got time to catch the 11:42 train. Goodbye.
Well, that's one person who's quite unconcerned by all this business.
Yes, but somehow he seems rather more preoccupied than usual.
Look out! Here he comes! Get the chloroform ready.

TOOT
'Morning Professor. Going to the village? ... Yes? ... Well, jump in.
By the whiskers of Kûrvi-Tasch! We've missed him!
Meanwhile . . .
. . . And that's the whole story, gentlemen. Can you make anything of it? . . . I just give up.
Hmm . . . We'll have to think this over.
All right. But there's just one thing: please don't gossip about this business. I don't want a whole crowd of sightseers here.
You can rely on us; "Mum's the word". That's our motto.
Yes, "Dumb's the word". That's our motto.
Good; thanks.
Next morning . . .
New York News
. . . AND NOW GLASSNIKS?
Daily Reporter
MYSTERY AT MARLINSPIKE
Famous Sailor in Glass Sensation
No clue has so far been found
ON DIMANCHE
Mystère du verre brisé
HAMBURGER TAGEBL
WAS IST LOS IN MARLINSPIKE?
GRANDE PANIC
FISH & CHIPS
SOUVENIRS OF MARLINSP
TV
A.TORTICOLLI

Just look at that horde of rubber-necks! They can hardly wait to see the rest of my windows smashed to bits!
No doubt. But somehow I think they are going to be disappointed.
What do you mean?
It's just a thought . . . By the way, I know Calculus hates anyone going into his laboratory, but I'd rather like to have a look round in there. Have you got his key?
Yes . . . but what's the idea?
Well, I've been thinking about this business, and one thing struck me; the glass-breaking only occurred when Calculus was out; or, to be more accurate, when he was in his laboratory. And since he left for Geneva yesterday, nothing more has happened.
In a nutshell, you suggest our friend Cuthbert's responsible for all those incidents? But that's ridiculous!
I'm not suggesting anything, Captain. I'm simply trying to work it out.
Sniff . . . sniff . . .
?
I say, Captain, can you smell anything?
Sniff . . . Sniff . . .
It's just . . . sniff . . . tobacco, that's all.
Yes, but Calculus doesn't smoke.
Blistering barnacles, that's quite right!

Stop him, Captain!
Whoa there, my fine friend!
Too late, confound it! He's got away!
Hello, what's this on the floor?
It's no use following him: he's disappeared . . . But look what fell out of his pocket when Snowy ripped it.
МАЗЕДОНИА
20
20
A packet of cigarettes and an ignition key. Well, we know something about him – and I know something else. He's got a punch like the kick of a mule!
Poor Captain!
And there's another thing. Look!
Broken glass! Blistering barnacles, you were right. It's certainly Calculus who . . .
HANDS UP!
?

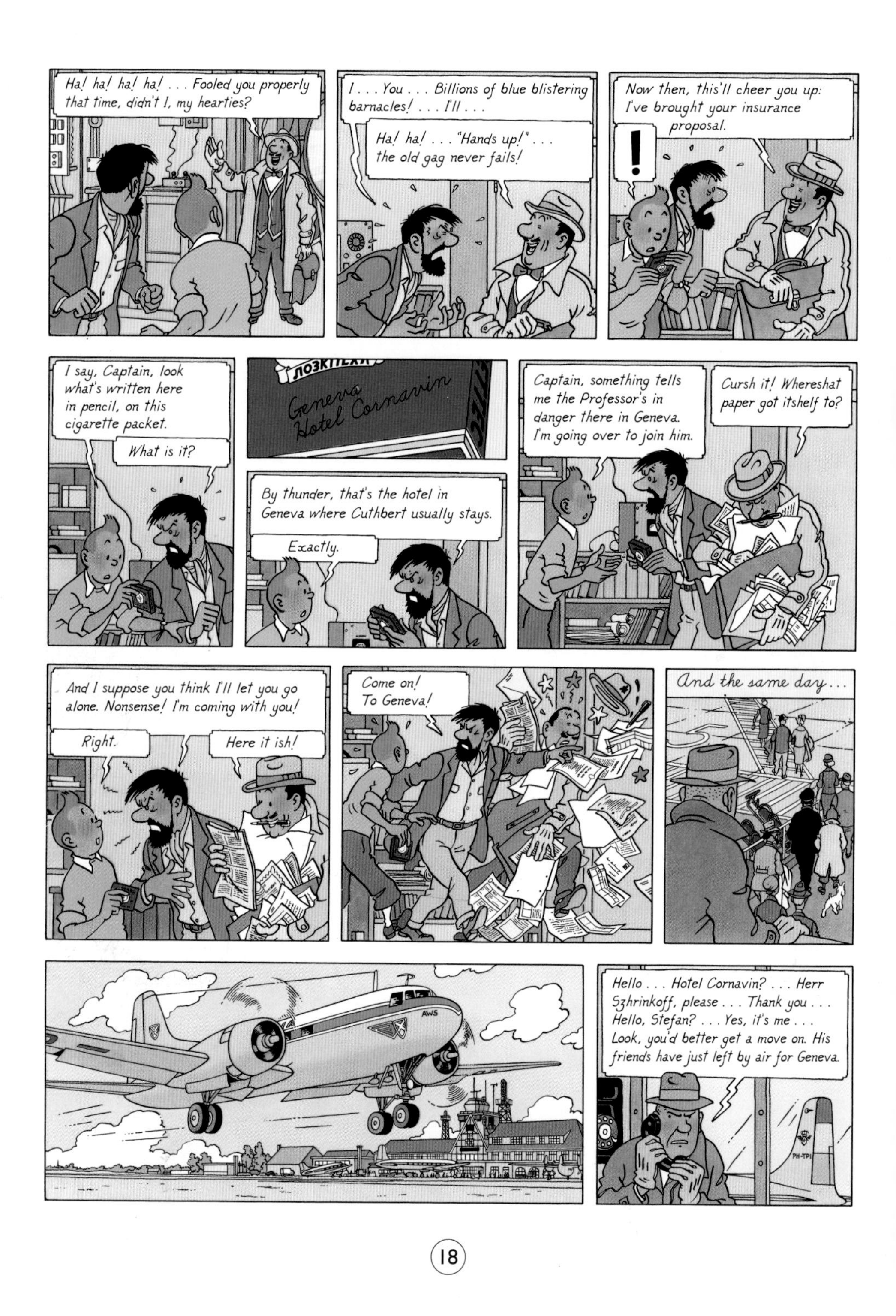
Ha! ha! ha! ha! . . . Fooled you properly that time, didn't I, my hearties?
I . . . You . . . Billions of blue blistering barnacles! . . . I'll . . .
Ha! ha! . . . "Hands up!" . . . the old gag never fails!
Now then, this'll cheer you up: I've brought your insurance proposal.
!
I say, Captain, look what's written here in pencil, on this cigarette packet.
What is it?
Geneva Hotel Cornavin
By thunder, that's the hotel in Geneva where Cuthbert usually stays.
Exactly.
Captain, something tells me the Professor's in danger there in Geneva. I'm going over to join him.
Cursh it! Whereshat paper got itshelf to?
And I suppose you think I'll let you go alone. Nonsense! I'm coming with you!
Right.
Here it ish!
Come on! To Geneva!
And the same day . . .
AWS
Hello . . . Hotel Cornavin? . . . Herr Szhrinkoff, please . . . Thank you . . . Hello, Stefan? . . . Yes, it's me . . . Look, you'd better get a move on. His friends have just left by air for Geneva.

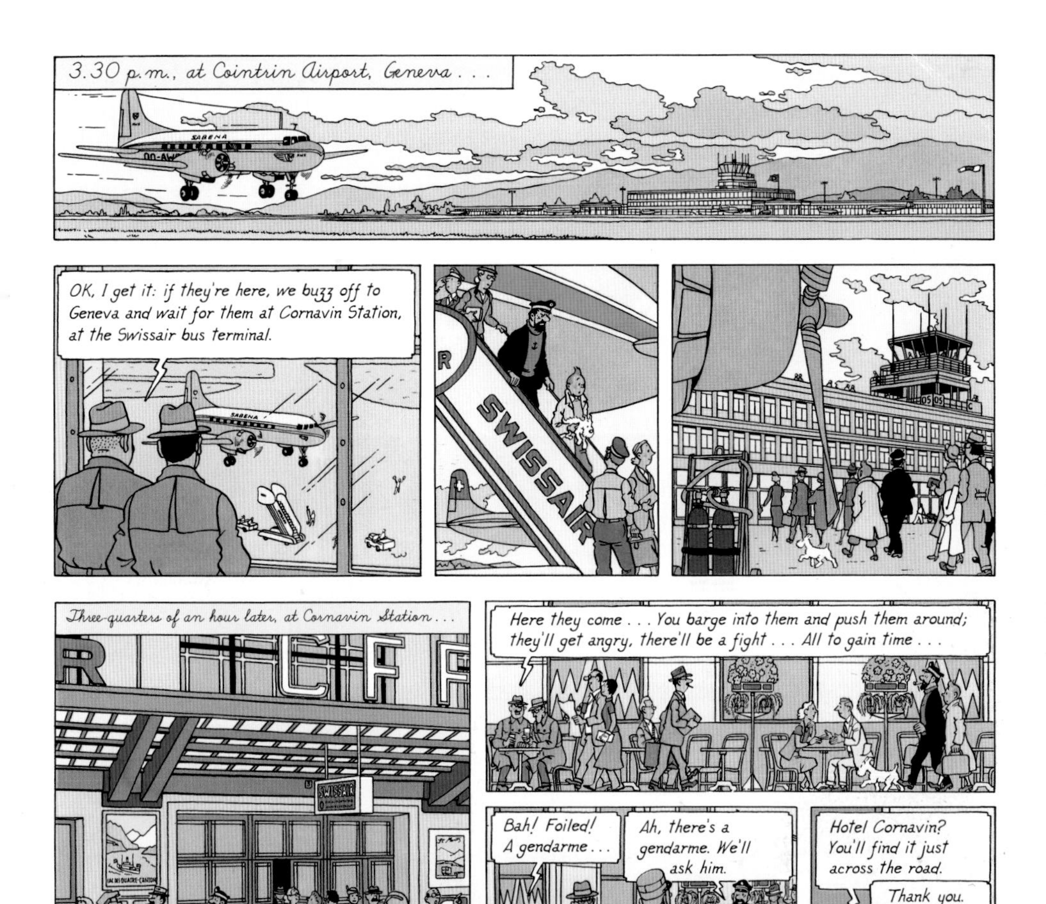
3.30 p.m., at Cointrin Airport, Geneva . . .
SABENA
OK, I get it: if they're here, we buzz off to Geneva and wait for them at Cornavin Station, at the Swissair bus terminal.
SWISSAIR
Three-quarters of an hour later, at Cornavin Station . . .
CFF
SWISSAIR
Here they come . . . You barge into them and push them around; they'll get angry, there'll be a fight . . . All to gain time . . .
Bah! Foiled! A gendarme . . .
Ah, there's a gendarme. We'll ask him.
Hotel Cornavin? You'll find it just across the road.
Thank you.

HOTEL
CORNAVIN
CORNAVIN

Is Professor Calculus staying here, please?
Professor Calculus? Yes, sir. His key is not on the board, so he must be in his room.

Phew, what a relief! Please tell him Captain Haddock and Tintin are here.
Certainly, sir.

What's up?
?
?

It's very odd . . . he isn't answering. Yet he should be in his room.
Perhaps he can't hear. We'd better go up. What number is his room, please?
Number 122, fourth floor. The lift is on your left.
Thank you. We'll leave our luggage here.
Fourth floor, please.
Certainly, sir.
LIFT
LIFT
LIFT
LIFT
Blistering barnacles, I know he's deaf . . . but all the same . . .
Supposing he's not in his room; supposing something's happened to him . . .
Not in his room, sir? Then his key should be here.
!
Great snakes! But there it is!
122
You're right . . . He must have gone out while my back was turned . . . I'm terribly sorry, sir.
You don't know where he might have gone?
Wait . . . I've got it. This morning Professor Calculus asked me for the time of trains to Nyon. I remember now: he said he'd take the 4:40. If you hurry you'll still catch him at the station.
Good. Thank you.
Look out! Here they come.
We have exactly seven minutes.

VOYAGES
Hey, you! Why can't you watch where you're going?!
You clumsy oaf, are you suggesting it was my fault?
What?! You have a nerve, insulting me, you blundering bargee!
Captain!
Me, a bargee!! Billions of blue blistering barnacles, I'd have you know . . .
Floundering about! You ought to be locked up!
Please Captain, please! We shall miss Calculus . . .
Lucky for you I'm in a hurry!
Ha! ha! He says he's in a hurry!
Yes, in a hurry, you ectoplasmic by-product! Otherwise . . .
!
What happened? . . . I forgot it was a revolving door, that's all . . . and I pushed rather hard.
Let's hope we'll be in time.
Carpathian caterpillar! Just wait till I see him again!
The train to Nyon? . . . You're too late, sir; look, it's just gone.

Billions of blue blistering barnacles! All because of that Balkan beetle . . . I can't think why I don't go back . . .
That's a good idea; we'll go back.
I'm going to have a few words with that...
No you won't! We've other things to attend to.
Did Professor Calculus make any telephone calls after his arrival? . . . One moment, please; I'll inquire.
Hello, switchboard. Has No. 122 made any outside calls since he arrived? No. 122, yes . . . To Nyon 9. 51. 03 . . . Twice? . . . Thank you very much.
Nyon 9. 51. 03.
Hello, inquiries? Could you please give me the name and address of the subscriber at Nyon 9. 51. 03. Yes, I'll hold on . . .
Hello, yes . . . Topolino, Alfredo . . . 57A, route de Saint-Cergue, Nyon . . . Thank you very much.
Could you take us to Nyon? 57A, route de Saint-Cergue.
OK, sir.
TAXI
Filtra
TAXI
Did you notice, Captain, that the chap we surprised in Calculus's laboratory and the one who tripped you up were wearing the same sort of raincoat?
Maybe . . .
Go on, Stefan. Overtake them!
TAXI
VD 6539
GE 7051
Good. Now then, a little swerve, and jam on the brakes . . . hard!
TAXI
Wham!
?
TAXI
GE 7051
Crumbs! . . . What's happening? . . . We're skidding . . .
HELP! . . . HELP! . . . HELP!

Look! One's just come up again.
And there's a boy, too!
The driver? . . . And Snowy?
Don't know. Didn't see.
BLUB BLUB
And Snowy?
No sign.
?
!
BLUB BLUB
WOOAH
Swan's dinner! I ask you!
I saw it all! The roadhogs! They swerved deliberately. If they'd wanted to push you into the lake they couldn't have done it better.
Ah, the driver's just come round.
Thank goodness . . . Look here, there's something I must ask you to do for me. Would someone please take us on to Nyon? It's terribly urgent. We'll leave our names with you, to give to the police.
Half an hour later . . .
Nyon
Here we are, gentlemen. This is Nyon. To reach route de Saint-Cergue you go through the tunnel and turn right.
Good. Thank you very much.
Here we are.
By the whiskers of Kûrvi-Tasch! It's them! . . . They escaped! Run them down, Stefan: and this time, don't miss!

LOOK OUT!
VD-6539
The Citroen 15 that pushed us into the lake!
Brutes! . . . Filibusters! . . . Nitwits! . . . Steam-rollers! . . . Abecedarians!
Come along, Captain! . . . Let's hope we can get there before it's too late.
Here we are.
RRRRING
What is it? Can you hear something?
Come and have a listen at this door.
CLANG CLANG
Yes, that's it . . . How peculiar . . .
You stay here; I'm going round to the back of the house.
No one there.
?
It sounds like something bumping against a pipe . . .
Let's have another try. Perhaps they didn't hear us.
RRRRING
Ah, that's stirred them up: the owner's awake at last.
Tintin! Tintin! Come back! There's someone here.
?

Come in quickly! . . . The back door was open; I got in that way.
Ssh! . . . Listen . . .
Not a sound now . . .
WOOAH! WOOAH!
!
Calculus's umbrella! . . . Well done, Snowy! This absolutely proves it; he certainly came here.
Let's hope we're not too late. Perhaps he's still about . . .
Not a soul . . . But what's that on the table?
A bottle and two glasses. Someone was expecting us.
Crumbs! Just look at this book!
Wait a moment while I fix the light; it's as dark as a dungeon in here with the shutters closed.
There, now we can see properly.
I say, Captain, this is extraordinary!
182 SUMMARY OF MORE IMPORTANT DEVELOPMENT WOR
Fig. 69. SOUND USED AS A WEAPON by means of large parabolic pro-
ectors. Research conducted near Lofer, Germany, under the auspices
Speer Ministry
Look! . . . That's the same as the queer machine we found in Calculus's laboratory.
What is that book, anyway?
German Research in World War II
Leslie E. Simon
It's by an American scientist: "German Research in World War II". . . . Captain, this is a stroke of luck.
Ha! ha! ha! In fact, you've put your head right into the lion's mouth . . .

You will pay dearly for your folly, Lawton, my friend! Ha! ha! ha! . . . At last we can settle our account . . .
The radio!
The radio! . . . You set it going when you plugged in the lamp.
It's useless to shout; that will do you no good . . .
Great snakes! . . . THAT CIGARETTE! . . . Another!
Well, what about that cigarette?
Look at the brand!
ЛЗЕДОН
See here; it's the same as the packet dropped in Calculus's laboratory by that intruder.
Blistering barnacles, so it is!
CLANG
CLANG
Listen . . . there it is again.
You were absolutely right, Captain: something's knocking against the central-heating pipes. Let's have a look in the cellar.
Careful . . . Go quietly: don't make a noise.
CLANG
CLANG
Ssh! . . .
How silly they are! They've forgotten Uncle Cuthbert's nice new brolly!
BANG
CLANG
BONG

BANG
BONG
CLING
CLANG CLANG
Sssh!
?
CLANG CLANG
Who are you?
Who am I? Sapristi! I'm Professor Topolino!
Yes, Professor Topolino. I've been brutally assaulted and thrown into the cellar! . . . Just wait till I see that monster Calculus again!
Calculus, a monster?!
Yes, Calculus! Do you know the scoundrel?
Sir, Calculus is our best friend, and I refuse to allow . . .
Oh, so he's a friend of yours. My heartiest congratulations! What delightful people you know. Anyway, who are you and what are you doing in my house?
Yes, we owe you an explanation. But shall we do that upstairs, when you have cleaned up a bit?
A quarter of an hour later . . .
To sum up. Last Thursday the first windows and glasses were broken.
And it's no joke. Imagine: you're holding a glass in your hand and suddenly . . .
Just a minute, Captain . . . On the same day we heard the shots in the park, and found a wounded man who vanished. The next day Calculus left for Geneva, and the glass-breaking stopped immediately.
The day after that, a masked man slipped through our fingers in Calculus's laboratory, leaving behind a cigarette packet. On this packet was written: Geneva, Hotel Cornavin. We were anxious for our friend's safety, so we set off for Geneva.
Yes, without even stopping for a drink . . .
At the Hotel Cornavin, we had a row with a strange man. On the way from Geneva, a black Citroen tipped us into the lake.
We had a drink there, all right! But not as good as your excellent Swiss wine!
Finally, just near here, the same black Citroen tried to run us down, and missed by inches. A few minutes later, we found you in your cellar.
Er . . . That coal dust made me dreadfully thirsty. . . . What about you?
As for the packet of cigarettes, do you know this brand?
The brand that Boris smokes!
OOOH!

Who is Boris?
Boris? He's my servant. He smokes very little, and only those cigarettes. He gets them direct from Borduria.
From Borduria? . . . Boris is a Bordurian? . . . Where is he?
He left for home yesterday evening. They sent a telegram. His mother has just been taken ill.
Oho! It's '53!
I think I'm beginning to understand. Yes . . . But what's your story, Professor?
Well, it's like this. About a month ago I had the first letter from Calculus.
Your wine has rare distinction.
He wrote to say that he was on the verge of a sensational discovery, in the field of ultrasonics. As I am a specialist in that subject, he sought my advice. Last week another letter arrived . . . He had succeeded.
But it seems that the consequences of his invention so alarmed him that he wished to talk to me. I arranged to see him today.
Er . . . This bottle was intended for him?
Exactly. But help yourself if you feel like it. . . . This afternoon Calculus arrived, a little earlier than I expected, and we began to chat . . .
Then I bent down to pick up some papers. I looked up, and there was Calculus, brandishing a cosh . . . Then I came to in the cellar, bound and gagged.
I've got it!
Oh, sorry! . . .
Not at all!
Do you know this man?
Never seen him. Who is he?
Calculus! The one and only Calculus! So it wasn't he who knocked you out; it was someone else, masquerading as the Professor. Meanwhile the real Calculus arrived . . .
You're sure the timing mechanism hasn't stopped?
Don't panic! Only a few seconds to go . . .
And Calculus did come here; his umbrella proves that . . . He was met by the man who knocked you out, and then pretended to be you.
Good health, Professor!
That's how it must have happened . . .
BOOOM
Up she goes! That's got rid of the whole bunch at one stroke!

A few minutes later . . .
DING-GLING-GLING-GLING
Help! Help! We're under here!
Are you hurt?
Don't know . . . Don't think so . . . But be careful.
There's enough damage been done already, without smashing this bottle!
But hurry up! There were three of us in the house, and a dog.
There! . . . Glug . . . Glug . . .
That's it . . . Now I can pass out!
Ah, here come the others . . . Injured?
They're all unconscious.
Were there any casualties?
Three; two looked in very bad shape.
Next morning . . .
Topolino were taken from the wreckage. Fragments of a bomb were found in the debris and foul play is suspected. The police have detained two men found loitering in the vicinity of the crime, questioning passers-by. These two men will appear before the examining magistrate this morning.
Meanwhile speculation is rife as to the motive behind this attack, and every effort is being made to discover why Professor Topolino's house should
Bring in the two men, sergeant.
Very good, sir.

In you go!
Here we are!
Gentlemen, the statements you made yesterday have been checked and confirmed. You will be released immediately. I must apologise for our mistake.
That's quite all right, Mr Magistrate. None of this would have happened if our credentials hadn't been stolen . . . with our luggage.
We're in Swiss disguise while we're searching for our friends Tintin and Haddock. We have important news for them.
You'll find them in the hospital, quite near here.
A little later . . .
Tintin and Captain Haddock? I'll take you to their room. You're just in time. They're getting ready to leave.
I say, how clean these hospitals are. Just look at the shine on the floors!
ZIIIIIIP
?
. . . Yes, important news. We caught him . . . the man in the park who was wounded, then vanished. He's Syldavian. But we can't get another thing out of him. He swears he was there "quite by chance".
Quite by chance . . . I'll bet he was. Thanks all the same. I'm terribly sorry you slipped up . . . We must be off to the police station. Goodbye for now.
. . . This is how I see it. Calculus had perfected an ultrasonic instrument, capable of destroying glass from a distance, glass and - who knows? whole buildings, tanks, ships . . . In short, a terrible weapon . . . In a letter to Topolino, Cuthbert described his work.
This letter was discovered by Topolino's servant, a Bordurian called Boris, who tipped off his country's secret service. But the Syldavian espionage got wind of the invention too, and sent an agent to Marlinspike. He stumbled upon his Bordurian rival, who shot him.
So far so good. Then Calculus arrives in Geneva, but we are close behind. And since we make life difficult for spies and kidnappers, they try to eliminate us. Right . . . The first thing is to find Calculus.
But where can he be? . . . Who knows what they have done with poor Cuthbert?
VD 54321
CD
Blue blistering barnacles! . . . A lighted cigarette! The fat-headed fire-raisers!
Nit-witted ninepins! Bashi-bazouks! A "C.D." plate, so do as you like! Certified Diplodocuses, that's what you are!
OH!...

Look at this cigarette, Captain. The same brand . . . once again!
Thundering typhoons, you're right.
. . . It was a C.D. car . . . Diplomatic Corps. That means from an embassy, and most probably the Bordurian Embassy . . . We must find out where that is. A post office directory will tell us. We'd better go back to Nyon.
There . . . Bordurian Embassy, "Les Cygnes", Rolle.
Rolle . . . That's a few miles from Nyon.
Well then, this afternoon we'll reconnoitre. We'll go out to Rolle and spy out the land; and tonight, Captain, we'll go into action!
That night . . .
PCHH
Blood-suckers!
PCHH
Man-eating pests!
PCHH
PCHH
Lucky I brought this along!
PCHH
Don't make a sound Captain, we're nearly there.
PCHH
BZZZ BZZZ BZZZ
Wait, just a few more shots!
PCHH
BZZRRBZR
Here comes an absolute whopper! Listen to the din!
PCHH
OH! . . . Sorry!
He's landing on the lawn . . . Moor the boat and we'll have a look.
Look over there; someone's coming.
Crumbs! The man in the middle . . . no mistaking that silhouette . . . It's Calculus! They're going to put him aboard the helicopter!
Good heavens! What's happening?

Someone's trying to rescue Calculus! Quick, Captain, let's give them a hand!
I'm with you! Come on!
. . . But how can we tell friends from enemies?
Go for the ugliest . . . That won't be difficult - you'll see.
Now which has the ugliest mug? It looks about fifty-fifty . . .
Tintin! Is it really you? I can't believe my eyes!
Next please!
It's the thug who knocked me out in Calculus's laboratory, back at Marlinspike . . . the man with the cigarettes!
Quick, Captain, come on!
Rapp! . . . Noh dzem bûthsz!
Half a mo' . . . I'm coming . . .
PCHH
My umbrella! . . . My umbrella!
My umbrella!
The Captain . . . we must wait for the Captain . . .
Here I come!
The brutes! They've knocked out Tintin!

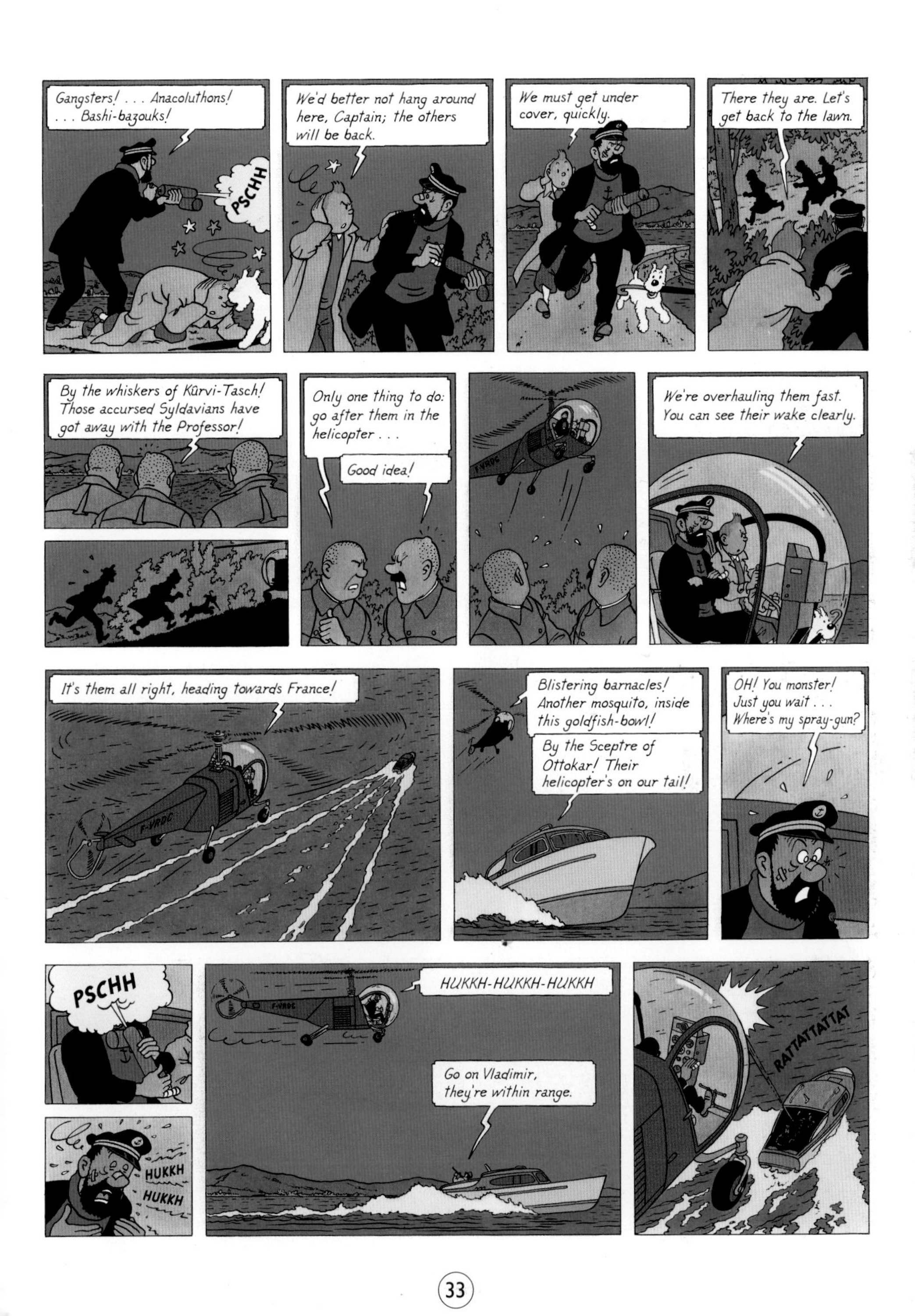
Gangsters! . . . Anacoluthons! . . . Bashi-bazouks!
PSCHH
We'd better not hang around here, Captain; the others will be back.
We must get under cover, quickly.
There they are. Let's get back to the lawn.
By the whiskers of Kûrvi-Tasch! Those accursed Syldavians have got away with the Professor!
Only one thing to do: go after them in the helicopter . . .
Good idea!
We're overhauling them fast. You can see their wake clearly.
It's them all right, heading towards France!
Blistering barnacles! Another mosquito, inside this goldfish-bowl!
By the Sceptre of Ottokar! Their helicopter's on our tail!
OH! You monster! Just you wait . . . Where's my spray-gun?
PSCHH
HUKKH
HUKKH
HUKKH-HUKKH-HUKKH
Go on Vladimir, they're within range.
RATTATTATTAT

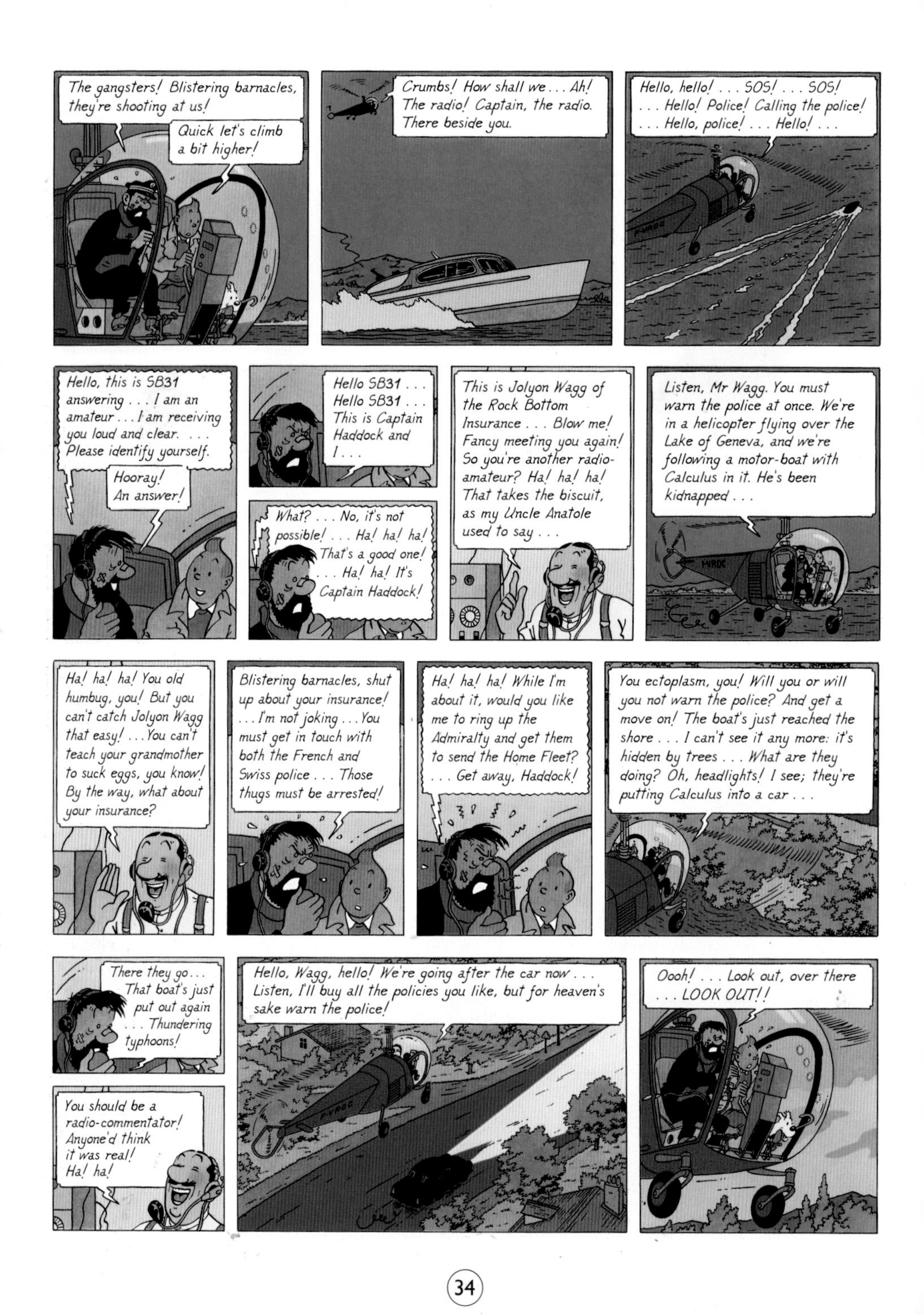

The gangsters! Blistering barnacles, they're shooting at us!
Quick let's climb a bit higher!
Crumbs! How shall we . . . Ah! The radio! Captain, the radio. There beside you.
Hello, hello! . . . SOS! . . . SOS! . . . Hello! Police! Calling the police! . . . Hello, police! . . . Hello! . . .
Hello, this is SB31 answering . . . I am an amateur . . . I am receiving you loud and clear. . . . Please identify yourself.
Hooray! An answer!
Hello SB31 . . . Hello SB31 . . . This is Captain Haddock and I . . .
What? . . . No, it's not possible! . . . Ha! ha! ha! That's a good one! . . . Ha! ha! It's Captain Haddock!
This is Jolyon Wagg of the Rock Bottom Insurance . . . Blow me! Fancy meeting you again! So you're another radio-amateur? Ha! ha! ha! That takes the biscuit, as my Uncle Anatole used to say . . .
Listen, Mr Wagg. You must warn the police at once. We're in a helicopter flying over the Lake of Geneva, and we're following a motor-boat with Calculus in it. He's been kidnapped . . .
Ha! ha! ha! You old humbug, you! But you can't catch Jolyon Wagg that easy! . . . You can't teach your grandmother to suck eggs, you know! By the way, what about your insurance?
Blistering barnacles, shut up about your insurance! . . . I'm not joking . . . You must get in touch with both the French and Swiss police . . . Those thugs must be arrested!
Ha! ha! ha! While I'm about it, would you like me to ring up the Admiralty and get them to send the Home Fleet? . . . Get away, Haddock!
You ectoplasm, you! Will you or will you not warn the police? And get a move on! The boat's just reached the shore . . . I can't see it any more: it's hidden by trees . . . What are they doing? Oh, headlights! I see; they're putting Calculus into a car . . .
There they go . . . That boat's just put out again . . . Thundering typhoons!
You should be a radio-commentator! Anyone'd think it was real! Ha! ha!
Hello, Wagg, hello! We're going after the car now . . . Listen, I'll buy all the policies you like, but for heaven's sake warn the police!
Oooh! . . . Look out, over there . . . LOOK OUT!!

A pylon! Power cables!
We just missed them. But blistering barnacles, we're out of control!
Whew! We're safe!
I think we must have trimmed the treetops.
Ha! ha! ha! Still keeping up the commentary! You know, you're an absolute wow at the mike, Captain!
You prize purple jellyfish, you! Must I kill myself drumming it into your thick skull? This is no joke! . . . Now listen to me, Wagg . . .
Don't bother, Captain; it's too late anyway. Look: the petrol gauge is down to zero. A bullet must have holed the tank. The only thing we can do is to land on the road in front of the car and force it to stop.
Help!! She's misfiring!
PTTT
PTTT
PTTT
!
!
?
No, the engine's picked up.
Quick! Down on the road!
That's it!
!
There they are! BUT . . . ?!
D 25
CERVENS
5,2 Km.

Thundering typhoons! They must have a Jack Brabham at the wheel!
That's that. They've slipped through our fingers . . . And Calculus with them.
Now what'll we do?
First we'd better clear the road, in case of accidents.
Then continue on foot . . . and try to hitch-hike.
Ah! A car . . . Let's thumb a lift.
Blackguards! . . . Egoists! . . . Nitwits! . . . Troglodytes! . . . Polygraphs! . . .
It's incredible what cads some drivers are. They see you like that, all alone on the road, and whoosh! . . . they sweep past! Blistering barnacles, what times we live in!
Hey, here comes another.
Beasts! . . . Autocrats! . . . Profiteers! . . . Fat faces! . . . Tramps! . . .
There ought to be a law to make those infernal mileage-merchants stop when people signal.
Ah, another. Let's try again.
Bah, they won't stop. You'll see.
I say, they've stopped.
TSIIIII
Oh well, we needn't despair. There are still a few gentlemen left in the world.
Tintin! . . . Wait! . . . STOP! . . .
?

Quick! Into the wood . . .
Hurry! . . .
Get down: like me.
Why in that particular puddle?
SPLOSH
I say, Captain, what are you doing?
Blistering barnacles, get down! They'll start shooting any moment! Didn't you recognise the black Citroen?
The black Citroen? . . . No, Captain, you've got it wrong. It was black all right, but it had a French number plate: the other one was Swiss.
Are . . . are you quite sure?
Absolutely certain. Come on, perhaps they're still there.
But I promise you, my pet, there were two people in the road who signalled to me.
And I say, Jules, that it's time you went to the oculist and ordered stronger glasses.
And on top of it all, you're soaked . . .
Oh, the sun will soon dry me off.
Hmm! I wouldn't count on it.
If only we had an umbrella!
An umbrella? Captain, what idiots we are. Look!
?

. . . Yes, and meanwhile poor Calculus is being whisked further and further away!
TABAC
At last! There's a tobacconist. I'm going to buy an ounce or two.
You go on. I won't be a minute.
TSHHH
!
BANG
HELP! . . .
Oh goodness! How awful! Poor Captain! What a ghastly thing to happen!
Bandit! . . . Anthropophagus! . . . Steam-roller! . . . Highwayman! . . . Travelling at that speed! I suppose you want to break the sound-barrier? You thundering misguided missile, you!
Bashi-bazouk! . . . Ectoplasm!
Mamma mia! It was you! . . . Basta! . . . And now why you spitta all over my window?
Presto! Window-wash!
Eccolà!
Excuse me, sir, but could you please help us? We're chasing some car-bandits . . . they've kidnapped one of our friends, Professor Calculus, and . . .
Madonna! . . . Uno bandito . . . we chase? Va bene! You get in my car . . .
You in good?
OK.
SLAM
BRRROOM
Avanti!
Billions of blue blistering barnacles! Must you do that? Can't you start off like other people?
Scusi!
I show you . . . Italian car, Italian driver, the best in the world, no? Avanti! Prestissimo! We catcha him, il povero Professore!

Perhaps we'd better explain. Our friend Calculus has an invention which secret agents from a foreign power are trying to steal. That is why they kidnapped Calculus.
But a rival gang, probably secret agents from another country, grabbed our friend.
Hitch-hikers! Blistering barnacles, there ought to be a law against them!
As I was saying, this second gang snatched our friend from the first lot. We . . . er . . . Don't you think we'd better slow down?
DANGER WET TAR
!
Mamma mia! . . . Whatta is happening? This noise is peculiare. Diavolo! I think now: uno pistone? . . . Una valvola?
CLICK
CLICK
CLICK
CLICK
CLICK
CLICK
CLICK
It . . . it . . . it's nothing. . . . It . . . it . . . it's my . . . my t-t-t-teeth . . . ch-ch-ch-ch-chattering . . .
Olà! You think I drive troppo presto?
Er . . . I believe the Captain thinks that you're flying too low . . .
CLICK
?
Ten thousand thundering typhoons! Must you drive like a lunatic?
There it is! That car there! The Chrysler that's just gone through the village.
30
HELP! . . .

Whew! ... Passed it!

Blistering barnacles, just our luck! It's market day!

BAR
MAIRIE

Hey! A gendarme!

You barbarian! Going through a built-up area at that speed! You'll pay for this! . . . Your name?

Arturo Benedetto Giovanni Guiseppe Pietro Archangelo Alfredo Cartoffoli da Milano.
Er . . . I . . . Hm . . . Well, don't do it again . . .
VRROOM
Now we make up for the lost time . . . Avanti!

Blistering barnacles, we'll break our necks, I tell you!
There they are again!
Bene! Bene! We catcha them up!
Thundering typhoons! The level-crossing barrier's closing. We're too late to get through.
ZZINGG
ZZINGG
Whew! Thundering typhoons, if we go on like this I'll have a heart attack!
. . . Now, we give a nice little swerve, so! . . .
. . . We put on the brakes, so! . . . Ecco! . . . Superbissimo!
That's odd. I can't see Calculus . . .
By heaven!! What d'you think you're playing at? What do you want?
What do we want? Quite simply: Calculus. Where is he?
Calculus? And what might that be: Calculus? A plant? An animal? A chemical?
You know as well as we do! What have you done with him?
I'd ask you to mind your manners. Once and for all, I've never heard of your Candyfloss! You can see that my chauffeur and I are alone in my car . . .
What about the boot?
Young man, I could say that the contents of my boot are none of your business: but since I don't wish to be nasty . . .
There! Now where's your Coelacanth? Inside the spare wheel, I suppose.

Does that satisfy you, Mr Sherlock Holmes? Or would you like to dismantle my carburettor? No? In that case, get out of the road and let me pass. You've wasted enough of my time already.
I . . .
But . . .
Mamma mia! You fool me nicely, yes? . . . You tella me the big fib, yes? You just wanta to make hitch-hike . . . and me stupido who believes you! Madonna, how you fool me! Va bene! Now you walk. Addio!
What can have happened? Did we follow the wrong car? . . . Or did Calculus stay in the motor-boat? . . .
GREAT SNAKES!
Hey, what's the matter? Now what's burning you up?
YEOW!
What idiots we are! Under the back seat!
Why? . . . What? . . . Which back seat?
It was rather high up . . . That's where they've hidden poor Calculus! We let ourselves be hoodwinked like a couple of kids. Come on!
Old Calculus has certainly led us a pretty dance around the countryside!
That aeroplane looks as if it's landing. Is there an airfield near here? If that's the case, we're saved.
Come on, let's take this footpath. When we get to the airfield we'll ask if there's a plane available.
What's all this? . . . No airfield? . . . It's come down in a meadow.
Look! There, behind those trees!
The Chrysler!!

There's Calculus! They're putting him aboard the plane. Quick Captain!
By St. Vladimir! There are those madmen again!
Quick, Stanislas, climb aboard. And start up the engine, Boldoff; hurry! Too bad about the car: we'll abandon it.
Step on it, Boldoff!
SY-ONF
Faster! Faster!
What are you waiting for? Take off!
Ah! That's it!
At last! Calculus is ours!
Wooah! Wooah!
WOOAH!
YOW! OW! OW!
HELP! HELP!
?

SAVE ME!
Great snakes! Poor Captain!
Hurry, blistering barnacles! Help me!
A few minutes later . . .
Thundering typhoons, you were right! The back seat is hollow. The pirates! That's where they hid him!
Listen Captain, we mustn't waste time. It was a Syldavian aircraft: we'll go back to Geneva and take the first plane for Syldavia.
Right!
Next morning in Geneva . . .
While you buy the tickets I'll get some papers. Then I'll put a call through to Marlinspike . . .
SEE CLEARLY WITH BETTASPE
Two seats for Klow, sir? Certainly. The plane leaves from Cointrin in two hours' time.
Swissair
JOURNAL DE GENEVE
BLISTERING BARNACLES!
Incredible! . . . Fantastic! . . . That's upset the apple-cart!
CHANGE
WECHSEL
EXCHANGE
!
?
You Carpathian Bashi-bazouks! That's the second time you've crossed my path. I hope for your sakes there won't be a third. You two-timing Tartar twisters, you! . . . Understand? . . .
Just remember, I've got my eye on you!
SEE CLEARLY WITH BETTASPECS

Hello! What's happened to you?
Er . . . nothing . . . a slight mishap. But read this; it's incredible.
BORDURO-SYLDAVIAN INCIDENT
Bordurian fighters force down Syldavian plane
"VIOLATION OF OUR AIR-SPACE"
SAYS SZOHÔD
A Bordurian Air Ministry communiqué reports that a Syldavian aircraft has been intercepted by fighters while flying over Bordurian territory. Despite repeated warnings,
"UNPROVOKED TASCHIST AGGRESSION"
KLOW PROTESTS
In an official note the Syldavian Ministry of Foreign Affairs has protested vigorously against "unprovoked aggression by the Bordurian Air Force towards an unarmed
Great snakes! This alters everything. I bet that's the plane Calculus was in. Now he's fallen into Bordurian hands again. They never give up, do they?
Your tickets for Klow, sir.
We don't need them! We're going to Szohôd, in Borduria.
Yes . . . er . . . Can we by any chance . . .
I'm sorry, sir, the flight to Szohôd is fully booked. The last two seats have just been taken. However, if you would care to wait . . .
. . . we may have a last-minute cancellation. In that case we can make arrangements for you.
By the whiskers of Kûrvi-Tasch! They want to go to Szohôd, you can bet your life. But we took the last two seats. I wonder . . .
You'll wait here? Good. I'm just going to see if I can get through to Marlinspike.
All right.
Yes, Marlinspike 421. Thank you, I'll hold on.
Hello? . . . Hello, Marlinspike? Hello, is that you, Nestor? . . . What? . . . Who's that speaking? . . .
Cutts the butcher speaking . . . What can I do for you? . . . Hello?
Hello, operator. That was the wrong number. I asked for 421 . . . Yes, 421.
Hello? Hello, is that 421? Is that you, Nestor? This is Captain Haddock. I . . . Who is that speaking? . . . Who?!
Wagg . . . Jolyon Wagg . . . Proper lark this is, eh? You old humbug, you didn't half give me a laugh with your helicopter chase . . . What? . . . What am I doing here?
It turned out nice, so I brought the wife for a little visit to your country seat . . . Yes . . . Who? . . . Nestor? . . . I'll hand you over to him; he's got a good joke to tell you . . . Hi, Nestor, it's your boss.
Hello . . . Ah, Nestor, how are you? . . . Yes . . . No . . . Perhaps . . . And what's your news at Marlinspike?
WHAT?

I'm afraid it's the truth, sir. The Professor's laboratory has been stripped . . . Yes, the apparatus too, sir . . . Absolutely everything . . . Quite so, last night. Yes, sir, the police came this morning.
Did they find any clues? . . . You . . . Hello? . . . What did you say, Nestor?
No, it's me, Wagg . . . Don't worry, old boy; it's better than a slap in the eye with a wet kipper, as my Uncle Anatole used to say. Besides . . .
Thundering typhoons! Shut up about your Uncle Anatole and put me back to Nestor, or I'll do something desperate!
Right away . . . You know, your insurance is ready. And you'll see, I've taken care of everything. You've got the lot: theft, fire, hailstorms, air-disasters . . .
Wagg! Billions of bilious blue blistering barnacles! I . . . Hello! . . . hello! . . . HELLO!
Now I've been cut off! ! . . .
I say, what's the matter now?
What's the matter? It's Calculus's laboratory at Marlinspike! Rifled! emptied! ransacked! Those gangsters have taken all his apparatus . . .
And when I think they're probably in league with those two Patagonian savages . . . Hello, they've weighed anchor.
So they have: they've gone.
Excuse me, sir! . . . Sir! . . . Sir! . . .
Someone's just telephoned: we have two vacant seats on the plane for Szohôd . . . but the coach leaves in five minutes. Will that be . . .
Thanks, we'll take them.
A few minutes later . . .
HOTEL BEAUJOLAIS
CAFE DES CHEMINS DE FER
SWISSAIR
Bon voyage, gentlemen. We're only too delighted to give you our seats . . .
You're the last, sir. We're just off now.
ISSAIR
ZOHOD
!

Right away, François.
SWISSAIR
Well done Snowy! He's been to fetch Calculus's umbrella.
GENEVE
Crumbs! This doesn't belong to Calculus. Snowy! Where in the world did you pinch this from?
Thundering typhoons! Quick, Tintin, hand me that brolly.
Hey, I think you've lost your umbrella! Here it is.
Hello, what's that on my nose?
Oh, it's the bit of sticking-plaster.
It's off now . . .
Thundering . . .
. . . typhoons!
!
?
Pardon me, but you have something on your hat.
A bit of sticking-plaster.
Now I wonder where that came from?
It's sticky! . . .
And it's stuck!
Oh, bother it!
Ah, it's gone.
Well, that's got rid of that!

At Cointrin Airport, 1.40 p.m.
Here we go, on our way to Szohôd . . . I only hope we find poor Calculus there.
Billions of bilious blue blistering barnacles!
Just look at this confounded sticking-plaster! How did it get itself on to my cap? It's black magic, I tell you!
Meanwhile, in Geneva . . .
Hello, operator, I want Szohôd 322.18 . . . Yes, Szohôd . . . What? A delay? But it's urgent. I . . . Good. Try and hurry things along.
Hello? . . . Hello? . . . Yes, I can hear you . . . CRACKLE . . . FRRT . . . Hello, Szohôd? Hello, I . . . FRRT . . . Hello?
2.17 p.m.
2.35 p.m.
Hello? Yes, I can hear you . . . Hello? . . . GLOUIP . . . CRR . . . Will you . . . Hello? . . . What? . . . Ah, it's you, Szhrinkoff. Amaïh! . . . CRRR . . . Hello?
2.52 p.m.
3.03 p.m.
!
Hello? . . . FRRWT . . . Hello, I can't hear you CLACK . . . What? . . . FRRT . . . CRRACK . . . Can't you speak up?! . . . What?
3.48 p.m.
Yes, Haddock. A sort of sea-dog with a beard . . . CLACK . . . BZZ . . . Beard . . . HIIP . . . No, beard . . . GRR . . . He has a beard! . . . XWUUI . . . XWUUUI . . . Yes beard!
4.30 p.m.
SZOHÔD
Hello! CRACK . . . Yes, I've got it . . . CRACK . . . FRR-RRT . . . By the whiskers of Kûrvi-Tasch, what a line! . . . Captain Haddock and Tintin: OK, OK. I'll warn the airport control at once . . . Amaïh!
SZOHO
TZHÔL - DOUANE - CUS
Hello, airport police here . . . Amaïh Kûrvi-Tasch, sir! The plane from Geneva? It's just in . . . What? . . . What names?
AMAIH
KSZY-GU

That's a relief, I can tell you. I thought they might have had warning of our arrival.
SZTÔPP!
?
!
NG
You Captain Haddock? And you Tintin? . . . You come please. My officer want talk with you.
What? Who is this officer of yours?
Captain, wait. You've got something . . .
A few minutes later . . .
Ah, Captain, this is a great privilege for us. We in Borduria salute you, hero of that glorious interplanetary flight . . . Amaïh!
And you too, Mänhir Tintin. I am proud to shake the hand which . . . er . . . first set foot on the Moon. I salute you. Amaïh!
You . . . You're too kind.
The ancient traditions of Bordurian hospitality demand that we ensure your absolute comfort and safety.
Szplug! What is this?
As I was saying: your safety . . . Two interpreters will therefore accompany you during your stay here. They will take you wherever you may wish to go . . . and at whatever time.
These gentlemen, Krônick and Klûmsi, are entirely at your service . . . They will take you to the Hotel Zsnôrr, where rooms are booked for you. I wish you a pleasant stay . . . Amaïh!
Thanks . . . very much.
Ten minutes later, in Szohôd . . .
. . . And this is Kûrvi-Tasch Platz. Your hotel is just round the corner.
HOTEL ZSNÔRR
Here we are. This is it.
One moment, please. We'll see about your rooms.
Be careful! Those two ostrogoths in Geneva certainly tipped off the police here. We must keep our eyes open.
Oh! . . . Quick! . . . Hide! Hide!

BIANCA CASTAFIORE!!!
Did you see? That was Signora Bianca Castafiore, the Milanese nightingale. She's singing at the Szohôd Opera. If you wish, we will go to hear her one evening: she is sublime as Marguerite, in "Faust".
Oh yes . . .
Here are the keys. We will escort you to your rooms.
This is yours, Mänhir Captain. I hope you will be comfortable.
Yours is a little further down: unfortunately there were no adjoining rooms.
Here you are, Mänhir Tintin. We will come and fetch you for dinner, in an hour. If you need us before then, don't hesitate to ring: we're entirely at your service.
Thank you, gentlemen.
We're prisoners all right, Snowy, and no mistake about it. The fact that it's a gilded cage doesn't make any difference.
Golly! The lap of luxury!
RRING RRING
Hello? . . . Oh, it's you, Captain . . . What?
Blistering barnacles, I said that at the first opportunity we'll ditch those two coleoptera! That's agreed, isn't it?
I . . . er . . . Oh yes. You're referring to those two butterflies you caught by the lake, in Geneva. But those aren't coleoptera, Captain, they're lepidoptera.
What are you jabbering about? Lepidoptera? Lepidoptera to you, too! I . . . Hello? . . . Hello?
Crumbs! How can I make him understand that our telephone is bound to be tapped?
CLICK
RRING RRING
Hello? . . . Yes . . . Yes . . . We were cut off. I . . . er . . . Don't worry about the butterflies, Captain . . .
Let's talk about the simply wonderful hospitality of this exquisite country. What good taste! What tact! And then their . . . um . . . their courtesy. And above all their . . . how shall I put it? their friendliness. Friendliness which is entirely . . . er . . . friendly . . . Um . . .
You . . . But . . . What . . . Let . . . But . . . Look here . . . I . . . Blister . . . Thunder . . .
Keep on recording. This could be interesting.
Ten thousand thundering typhoons! . . . Now I'm going to chuck you out of the window!

What? . . . No, blistering barnacles! It's that thundering bit of sticking-plaster. It's following me about!
Well, good luck. I'll leave you to sort things out together. But don't forget, we go down to dinner in an hour.
An hour later . . .
Captain, I propose we crack a bottle of champagne in honour of these gentlemen.
Champagne?! Champagne for this gang?
OWW!
Oh, poor Captain! It must be your rheumatism. Well, there's nothing like champagne for curing that. Will you call the wine-waiter?
Gentlemen, a toast to Borduria and her glorious ruler, Marshal Kûrvi-Tasch!
Amaïh Kûrvi-Tasch!
Amaïh Kûrvi-Tasch!
An hour later . . .
I say, they're having quite a party at table seven. That's their fourth bottle!
Ha! ha! I'm no fool! . . . You want to make us tight . . . To find out where . . . hic . . . Professor Calculus is . . . Hic . . . But you won't learn a thing. We'll shut up like trams . . . No, like prams . . . like lambs . . . no, like clams . . .
Don't let's worry about Calculus. He'll have to shift for himself.
That's right! Hic . . . Don't let's worry. Anyway . . . hic . . . I don't know anything. Honestly . . . It's Sponsz . . . hic . . . the Chief of the "ZEP" . . . our secret pol . . . hic . . . he's the only one who knows . . . And Calculus . . .
Good . . . good. Let's forget silly old Calculus. It's time for bed.
Will you take us right up to our rooms?
Hic . . .
I . . . hic . . . I'll stay in the corridor.
Fine . . . Good idea!
OK. Mine's locked in your room.
And mine in yours.
THUMP
THUMP
THUMP
THUMP

Thundering typhoons! He'll rouse the whole hotel.
Wait. I'll open the door and we'll see . . .
THUMP
Hic . . . Not gone to bed yet? . . . I just wanted . . . hic . . . to give you your cap . . . Hic . . . Now, I'll stay in the . . . hic . . . corridor. I'll be . . . hic . . . very comfortable; they've put a bed there.
112
BANG
That's it! . . . Now then, let's go . . .
Crumbs! Get back, quick!
?
Get inside! And hurry!
Disgustingly drunk . . . That's why I telephoned the ZEP immediately.
You did well. All the exits are guarded.
Whew! They've gone.
Did you hear?
Wait. Perhaps over here . . .
Saved! It's the fire-escape!
Blistering barnacles! We're trapped!
What'll we do? . . . Ah, I think I've got an idea.
All right, Captain! . . . Ready?
HOTEL ZSNÔRR
ZSERVÍZ
BANG

This is it! . . . Come on!
A broken light-bulb! But where can that have come from?
HI!!
SZTÔPP!
Quick! The lights are still green!
SZARM
Meanwhile . . .
Yes gentlemen, we of the High Command are assembled today to hear about a remarkable discovery. After protracted research, Bordurian scientists have succeeded in perfecting a weapon . . .
. . . that will soon make H-bombs and ballistic missiles as obsolete as pikes and muskets! . . . The day is not far off, gentlemen, when this weapon will make the people of Borduria, and their glorious ruler Kûrvi-Tasch, masters of the world . . . To prove this to you, I invite you to give your undivided attention to this screen.
Here, challenging the world with its gigantic skyscrapers, is a great trans-Atlantic city, which it is superfluous to name.
Gentlemen, at our command, this city is doomed. In a few seconds it will be reduced to rubble. I have only to press this button . . .
So!
You see those proud buildings swaying on their foundations; they are cracking, disintegrating, toppling . . .
. . . and crumbling to dust. A whole city is wiped from the face of the earth!

Extraordinary!
Amazing!
Splendid!
We must keep calm, gentlemen! And above all, we must be patient. The great city which you saw disintegrating before your eyes was, for the time being, no more than . . .
. . . this model of glass and china . . . Yes, I can see the bitter disappointment on your faces: you are sorry not to have witnessed the actual destruction of a real city! Have faith, gentlemen!
This miniature city was destroyed from a distance by the machine you see here. It is an ultrasonic instrument. Up to now it is only effective against glass and china . . .
But in the near future we shall be able to destroy AT LONG RANGE not only glass and china, but bricks, concrete, and steel! The designs for this tremendous weapon already exist: that is all I can tell you at the moment . . . But when our hour strikes . . .
. . . then the enemies of Borduria will be stricken with terror before the might of our annihilating power . . .
Colonel, sir. You are wanted on the telephone.
Hello, Colonel Sponsz speaking . . . Oh, it's you Laszlo . . . What? . . . They've vanished! By the whiskers of Kûrvi-Tasch, it's impossible!
You lost track of them somewhere near the Opera? . . . Area surrounded? . . . Good . . . Well, as soon as I've finished here I'll trot along to the Opera and check the security precautions. And while I'm about it, I'll go and hear Castafiore.
An hour later, at the Szohôd Opera House . . .
Captain! . . . Wake up, Captain! It's the interval . . . Captain! . . .
You see, this is the safest place for us . . . No one could possibly guess that we'd taken refuge at the Opera!
It's true, Captain. When you're in a crowd there's always less chance of being noticed.

Just look, there's Colonel Sponsz, the Chief of Police.
So it is . . . Colonel Sponsz!
Sponsz, here! . . . And Calculus's fate depends on that man! Little does he know that he and his two henchmen passed within a yard of us!
RRRRRRRRRRING
It's the end of the interval. Shall we push off? . . .
I think it's better to wait till the end of the show. Then we can leave with the crowd.
An hour later . . .
It's hopeless! . . . The exits are stiff with policemen. Let's try to slip out through the stage door.
Why, look who's here! It's Tintin!
18
Hello, my dear young friend. How delightful to see you here.
Aha, you little flatterer, so you've come to congratulate me, with this . . . this fisherman . . . Mr? . . . Mr? . . .
Er . . . Hoddack . . . er . . . Haddad . . . Excuse me, Haddock.
Come into my dressing-room . . . Yes, yes . . . I can't leave my admirers in the passage . . . I've put on Marguerite's prettiest gown for you . . . Come along in.
You heard it? . . . Such a success, wasn't it? . . . One of the greatest triumphs of my career . . . What applause . . . especially for the Jewel Song . . . They were in ecstasies, weren't they, Mr Paddock?
Haddock, Madam!
RAT TAT TAT
Again? Ah, they won't leave me alone for a moment! . . . Oh well . . . Come in!
Signora, it's Colonel Sponsz, the Chief of Police. He wishes to pay his respects to you.
But of course! Show him in, girl . . .
? ?

Just a minute, Signora! . . . The Colonel . . . Listen, I'll explain everything later . . . but at all costs he mustn't find us here!
Dio! . . . What shall we do?
Irma, wait a moment! . . . Quick! Hide in my wardrobe, behind this curtain.
There . . . Show the Colonel in, Irmaa ♫ . . .
I am deeply honoured, Ma'am to . . . to find myself in the presence of the celebrated singer who . . . er . . . who . . .
Fie, Colonel! You make me blush!
But do please sit down.
You are too kind . . .
Oh, forgive me! . . . I've sat on something . . . It's a naval officer's cap . . .
Blistering barnacles! My cap!
!
I . . . Oh yes! . . . Er . . . it belongs to the tenor who sings in "Madame Butterfly" . . . He forgot it yesterday . . . But do take off your coat, Colonel.
With pleasure, Ma'am.
Take the Colonel's coat, please, Irmaa ♫ . . .
Now Irma, bring the champagne . . . It's an old habit of mine, Colonel: champagne after each performance. You'll take a glass with me?
I fear I intrude, Ma'am.
Not at all, not at all. Come, Colonel, make yourself useful . . . You may open the bottle.
But of course, Ma'am. Your wish is my command.
RAT TAT TAT
Come in.
Oh! Excuse me, Colonel . . . I . . . We were ordered to search the Opera House from top to bottom . . . For those two foreigners . . .
Is that so?

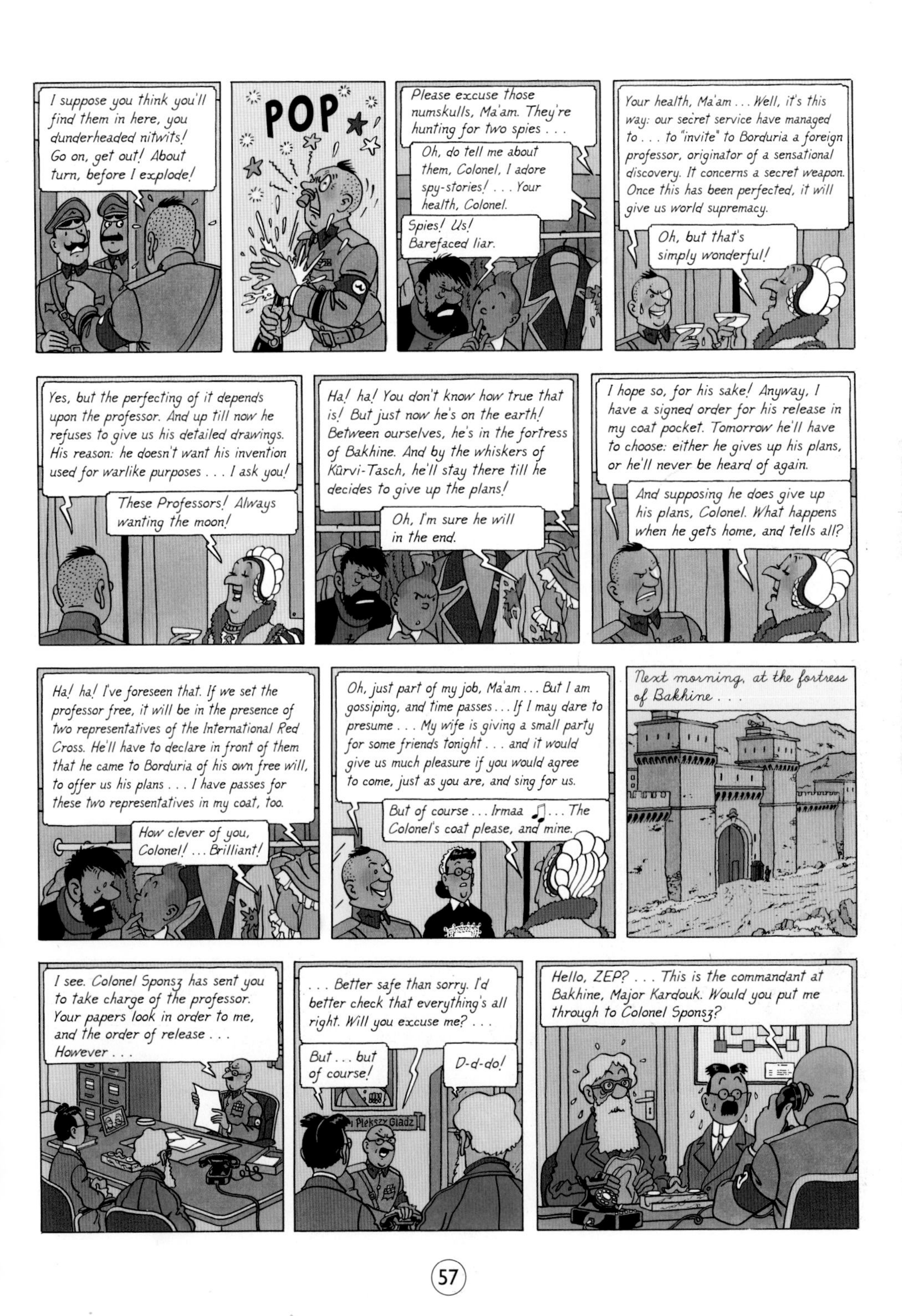
I suppose you think you'll find them in here, you dunderheaded nitwits! Go on, get out! About turn, before I explode!
POP
Please excuse those numskulls, Ma'am. They're hunting for two spies . . .
Oh, do tell me about them, Colonel, I adore spy-stories! . . . Your health, Colonel.
Spies! Us! Barefaced liar.
Your health, Ma'am . . . Well, it's this way: our secret service have managed to . . . to "invite" to Borduria a foreign professor, originator of a sensational discovery. It concerns a secret weapon. Once this has been perfected, it will give us world supremacy.
Oh, but that's simply wonderful!
Yes, but the perfecting of it depends upon the professor. And up till now he refuses to give us his detailed drawings. His reason: he doesn't want his invention used for warlike purposes . . . I ask you!
These Professors! Always wanting the moon!
Ha! ha! You don't know how true that is! But just now he's on the earth! Between ourselves, he's in the fortress of Bakhine. And by the whiskers of Kûrvi-Tasch, he'll stay there till he decides to give up the plans!
Oh, I'm sure he will in the end.
I hope so, for his sake! Anyway, I have a signed order for his release in my coat pocket. Tomorrow he'll have to choose: either he gives up his plans, or he'll never be heard of again.
And supposing he does give up his plans, Colonel. What happens when he gets home, and tells all?
Ha! ha! I've foreseen that. If we set the professor free, it will be in the presence of two representatives of the International Red Cross. He'll have to declare in front of them that he came to Borduria of his own free will, to offer us his plans . . . I have passes for these two representatives in my coat, too.
How clever of you, Colonel! . . . Brilliant!
Oh, just part of my job, Ma'am . . . But I am gossiping, and time passes . . . If I may dare to presume . . . My wife is giving a small party for some friends tonight . . . and it would give us much pleasure if you would agree to come, just as you are, and sing for us.
But of course . . . Irmaa ♫ . . . The Colonel's coat please, and mine.
Next morning, at the fortress of Bakhine . . .
I see. Colonel Sponsz has sent you to take charge of the professor. Your papers look in order to me, and the order of release . . . However . . .
. . . Better safe than sorry. I'd better check that everything's all right. Will you excuse me? . . .
But . . . but of course!
D-d-do!
Pleksy Gladz
Hello, ZEP? . . . This is the commandant at Bakhine, Major Kardouk. Would you put me through to Colonel Sponsz?

Hello? . . . What? . . . Oh, he's not in yet . . . Who is that? . . . His secretary? . . . In that case, perhaps you can help me . . .
Oh yes. Two representatives from the International Red Cross . . . Their passes? Quite all right, Major, I made them out myself. And the order for release? Yes, Major, that's quite all right too; the colonel signed it yesterday morning. Yes. Amaïh!
Well, gentlemen, everything's perfectly in order. I'll send for Professor Calculus.
A moment later . . .
Ah! The joy . . . popom-pom . . . pompity pom . . . pom
Here comes the chief. He sounds in good form this morning.
Amaïh! Kavitch . . . What's the news? . . . Any trace of Calculus's friends?
Nothing at all, Colonel. Not a sign of them.
That's tiresome . . . Very tiresome. I wonder where those two artful dodgers managed to hide . . . Nothing else, besides that?
Nothing at all, sir.
Oh yes . . . Major Kardouk rang up.
Kardouk? That old bore! And what did he want this time?
He wanted to know if the order you signed releasing Professor Calculus was official.
By the whiskers of Kûrvi-Tasch! When a document bears my signature, is it or is it not official?
Yes, Colonel. That's exactly what I told him, sir . . .
You . . . you did say the order releasing Professor Calculus?
Why . . . yes, Colonel . . .
?
!
The papers! . . . It's treason! . . . They've been stolen!
RRRING
Hello! . . . Yes, it's me . . . Amaïh! Colo . . . What? . . . Professor Calcu . . . But sir, I . . .
WHAT? . . . Their car's just gone? By all the hairs in the whiskers of Kûrvi-Tasch, if you don't get them back . . . I'll have you shot!

Yes, it's me, Haddock! . . . And there's Tintin, driving us to safety.
I'll tell you the whole story. The biggest joke is that Colonel Sponsz himself provided the means of your escape! . . . Magnificent, eh? And luckily it all happened at the Opera House; it only took a jiffy to find all we needed for disguises! Quite something, eh?
And my umbrella?
Yes, but don't start counting your chickens . . . It's two hours by car to the frontier, and if our little bluff is discovered before we're across . . .
CRACK
CRACK
What did I tell you? Motor bikes!
They've raised the alarm! That's bad . . .
Quick, Captain. Unclip the hood at the back. When you've done that, I'll let go at the front . . .
One!
Two! They're both down in the daisies!
Now, Captain; we were talking about my umbrella . . .
Saved for the moment; but I've a feeling that was only the first round . . .
OH! . . . How right I was! . . . Look there, a tank blocking the road! . . . Jam on the brakes!
We're skidding!
HELP! . . . HELP!

By the whiskers of Kûrvi-Tasch, they came a cropper!
If they're underneath that lot, there's not very much to be done . . .
BROOMM
A chance in a million! If we hadn't been thrown clear of the car . . .
Poor old Calculus is fearfully groggy . . . I say, Tintin, watch out! You'll have us in the ditch again!
I'm doing my best, but . . .
. . . I haven't driven a tank since our Moon trip.
Crumbs! . . . A road-block!
Too bad! I'll ram it.
What? . . . What's that you say? . . . A tank? . . . They've taken a tank!! Blow them up! . . . Exterminate them! . . . Pulverise them!! . . . I . . .
Trying to stop us with that kind of ramshackle erection!
Look out, here they come! . . . Don't miss! . . . FIRE!

BOM
I always told you this make of gun could be improved.
Hooray! He's coming round at last. Cuthbert! Cuthbert! It's me, old fellow . . . We're safe . . .
Ooh!
My umbrella! Have you got my umbrella?
Blistering barnacles, your umbrella! This is a fine time to worry about an umbrella!
Nonsense Captain! I'm talking about my umbrella. Surely you can't have lost it?
All right, I have lost your brolly . . . in Geneva, if you want to know.
That's good. I was hoping you hadn't lost it . . . You see, I hid my drawing . . .
Drawing? . . .
Boring? Of course it's not boring. I'm talking about the detailed drawings of my ultrasonic instrument, on microfilm. I hid them in the handle of my umbrella . . . So you see, if you'd lost it . . .
Hey!
I . . . What are all those things in the road?
MINES!
Too late! We can't stop in time! We'll blow up! HELP! . . . HELP! . . . HELP! . . .
By the whiskers of Kûrvi-Tasch! Who unloaded all that dud stuff on me? . . . It's sabotage!
Mines? . . . What are you jabbering about? We would have blown up. And talking of blowing up, I hope these things aren't dangerous. There's a case under my seat . . .
Those?
They're thunderflashes . . . used on exercises. When you light them, they explode with a terrific bang . . . Great snakes, it can't be true!
The frontier! We're coming to the frontier!
TZHÔL
Crumbs! . . . We're cornered this time!

A barricade! . . . With anti-tank defences on both sides! What shall we do?
Only one weak spot: the customs house itself! Here we go!
TZHÔL
HÔL
We're safe, Cuthbert!
Safe!
At last! Now I can have a quiet smoke to celebrate . . . the first since we set off.
The other frontier post. Nothing can happen to us now.
BOOOM
They must be refugees from the Kûrvi-Tasch regime . . . Poor devils! They'll be blown to bits.
Blistering typhoons! . . . I . . . I forgot all about them . . . those thundering thunder-things . . .
Two days later, in Geneva . . .
An umbrella, you say? Er . . . what sort of umbrella?
LOST PROPERTY
CRASH
BANG
CLANG
BOOM
Snowy! Here, Snowy!
My umbrella! My own little umbrella! At last I've found you!
And now watch carefully . . . I grasp the handle . . . I unscrew it . . . There . . . And hey-presto, what do we see? . . .
My plans!?!? Stars above! THEY'VE GONE!

But I'm quite certain that I . . . I can't believe it!
You believe what you like, but I've had all I can take! OK. You've been rescued; but your plans can look after themselves. I want to go home . . . to a little peace and quiet.
Two days later, at Marlinspike . . .
Ah, what a relief to be home again!
Thundering typhoons! What's going on here?
DADDY! . . . DADDY! . . . There's a great big man with a beard breaking my toys!
Look who's here! The ancient mariner himself! You dropped in just right, you old rascal: we were talking about you.
Billions of blue blistering barnacles! Wagg! What d'you think you're playing at?
Me? . . . Well, it turned out nice . . . But don't let us disturb you, old boy; make yourself at home . . .
It turned out nice . . . So I said: "Jolyon," I said, "don't you waste the end of your holiday." And your little place was vacant, so I popped in for a few days . . .
. . . with my little brood.
HERE! . . . QUICKLY!
It's Calculus; he went straight up to his room.

The microfilms! . . . I've found the microfilms! . . . I'd left them on my bedside table! Imagine me being so absent-minded!
Good old Cuthbert! . . . Well, now you'll be happy. I presume that without the plans the Bordurians really are in the soup?
No, no! On the bedside table.
And the cream of the joke is, without these plans the Bordurians can't do a thing! They're finished!
Only it's not just the Bordurians. It's everyone who wants to use my invention for warlike ends. And I shall never allow that. There's only one thing to do: destroy them all.
We mustn't dilly dally: the sacrifice must be made . . . Allow me, Captain.
PSCH
Billions of bilious blue blistering barnacles!
Oh! I'm so sorry! I didn't know . . . I thought . . .
Ten thousand thundering typhoons! My nerves won't stand much more of you. Every time I settle down, up pops trouble! . . . You flaming jack-in-a-box!
Chicken-pox?? . . . At your age? . . . Goodness!
Chicken-pox! . . . But that's very serious . . .
I say, old chum, I've just thought of something . . . all that clutter in your laboratory . . . is it insured?
Oh, I'm very well, thank you . . .
. . . but I'm very worried about the Captain: he has chicken-pox!
Chicken-pox? Well, that's nice for him.
Chicken-pox! Ha! ha! ha! Better go and live in a hen-coop! Ha! ha! ha! Chicken-pox! Ha! ha! ha!
Chicken-pox!!! But . . . but . . . it's infectious, chicken-pox is!!!
HERGÉ
THE END

HERGÉ

★

THE ADVENTURES OF

TINTIN

★

THE RED SEA SHARKS

LITTLE, BROWN AND COMPANY

New York Boston

THE RED SEA SHARKS

One evening, at the cinema . . .
THE END
Did you enjoy the film, Captain?
Oh yes . . . so-so, so-so.
The chap who played the lead is a good actor . . .
He looks like Alcazar; don't you think so?
THE OUT
. . . but the end was too improbable. The old uncle hasn't seen his nephew for twenty years . . . he starts thinking about him . . . the door opens, and hey-presto, who's there? The nephew!
It's as if I was thinking of . . . I don't know, someone or other . . .
DAMSAM
AVENUE
For example, take General Alcazar, whom you mentioned just now. He completely vanished from our lives years ago . . .
RTMAKE
AILOR
Well, d'you suppose, if I just think about him he'll pop up on the street corner, like that, bingo!?
!
Look here, you misguided missile, you! Can't you watch where you're going?
It's GENERAL ALCAZAR!
Caramba!

It's extraordinary! Imagine! The Captain and I were just this moment talking about you!
Qué? . . . Of me?
Yes, of you . . . weren't we, Captain? Then up you pop like a jack-in-a-box. It's incredible . . . But tell me, General, what are you doing nowadays?
Me? . . . Er . . . Well . . . Si . . . I . . . travel . . . But . . .
Por favor . . . excuse please . . . In mucho hurry . . . Already late for appointment . . . I go now.
Oh, what a pity . . . At all events, here's my address. And where can we find you, General?
Er . . . Um . . . At thees hotel . . . er . . . thees Hotel Bristol.
Good! The Bristol . . . And when do you . . .
Just so . . . Now I go . . . Adios, amigos!
Goodbye, General.
Well, well! Frankly, I don't think your friend Alcazar was in a very chatty mood!
Yes, an odd fellow. Oh well, come on.
?
OH!
Crumbs! It's the general's wallet. He didn't put it right inside his pocket.
Quick! He can't have got far.
Hello, where's he gone to? . . .
Perhaps he got into a car . . . Never mind. The Hotel Bristol is quite near; we'll leave his wallet there.
A few minutes later, at the Bristol . . .
General Alcazar? . . . No, Sir, we have no one of that name here.
BRISTOL

I wonder: perhaps he's registered under another name . . . Ramon Zarate? . . .
Ramon Zarate? . . . No, sir. A Spanish gentleman?
South American. Quite well-built. A long chin . . . small moustache . . . Wait, I'll try to draw him for you.
There . . . That's about it . . .
No, sir. I'm terribly sorry, but I don't know the gentleman.
Oh? That's odd. Well, thank you.
BRIST
Now what can we do to return that idiot's wallet to him?
That's what I'm wondering.
I say, why shouldn't the wallet itself give us a clue towards finding the general. Come on; we'll go in here.
Bring us . . . er . . . let's see . . . let's see . . .
Two glasses of ginger beer.
Now then, let's see what's inside here.
ROSSINI
Pound notes, French and Belgian money, a hotel bill, a four-leaf clover, a lottery ticket from San Theodoros . . . in fact, nothing to give us a lead.
CARLTON HO
LOTERIA NACIONAL
TARJETA
. . . And in this envelope, photos of aircraft . . . Odd, isn't it, Captain?
Ah, a letter! . . . This time I think we're on to something. Look, Captain.
Friday
Dear Sir,
Please telephone PIC 8524 between 10 and 12.0 p.m. Ask for Mr. Debrett
Regards, J.D.M.C.
But the general's address isn't here.
I know, but I'll ring up the number given in the letter.
ROSSINI
Hello, is that PIC 8524? May I speak to Mr Debrett? . . . Who am I? . . . A friend of General Alcazar, and I . . . Hello? . . . HELLO?? . . .

Can you hear me? . . . What? . . . You don't know the name Alcazar? . . . What about Ramon Zarate? . . . Nor that? . . . You see, sir, I found his wallet and . . . I beg your pardon?
I tell you, sir, I am not Mr Debrett! I don't know your General Alhambra, and I am not interested in your story . . . Goodbye!
There's politeness for you! . . .
Very odd . . . They don't know of him at that number. Too bad . . . We'd better be getting home to Marlinspike.
A little later . . .
How strange. The front door's open . . .
WOOAAAH! . . . WOOAAAH! . . .
?
?
Good heavens! My poor Snowy! Who's done this to you?!
I'll get to the bottom of it!
Hey, Captain, what's happened to you?
Billions of blue blistering barnacles! Who's the thundering son of a sea-gherkin who did that? . . . Nestor! . . . Nestor!
HAAAAH! . . .
Th . . . th . . . th . . . there behind you!
!?
RRHOAH! . . .

ABDULLAH! . . .
WRAOUH!
ABDULLAH? . . .
ABDULLAH! . . .
Abdullah! Blistering . . .
Again, Blistering Barnacles! Fall downstairs again!
You young ruffian! Just you tell me what you're doing here!
Wait! . . . Wait, Blistering Barnacles! I've got something for you.
Something for me?
Yes, a present.
A present! . . . Something specially for me, brought from his country, I expect. Dear little fellow!
It's for you, Blistering Barnacles, from me.
Thank you, Abdullah.
A cuckoo-clock! Why, it's magnificent, Abdullah!
You see . . . to wind it up . . .
. . . you do that!
Ten thousand thundering typhoons! . . . Don't think you'll get away with that!
WAAAH! WAAAH!
Halt thou! . . . Touch not the son of my Master!
?
?

Me Hassim, servant to His Highness Prince Abdullah . . .
And I bring you message from my Master.
Most esteemed and well-beloved friend,
I entrust to you my son Abdullah, to improve his English. Here the situation is serious. Should any misfortune befall me I count on you, my friend, to care for Abdullah.
Emir Ben Kalish Ezab
Read that, Tintin, it's for you . . . Tell me Hassim, what does the Emir mean . . . "the situation is serious"?
I know not, Effendi.
What d'you make of it? One thing's clear: we've got Abdullah on our hands. We'll have to bring the young scamp to heel.
Abdullah! . . . You little brat! I'm going to teach you a lesson . . .
WAAH!
Halt thou! . . . Touch not the son of my Master!
Touch not! Touch not! You arabesque, you! D'you imagine I'm going to let that little pest raise Cain in my house?
Just wait till I find you, you young rapscallion!
Oh sir! . . . Sir! . . . It's terrible, sir . . . All those foreign persons have settled themselves . . .
Later, Nestor . . . tell me later.
. . . in the state-rooms!

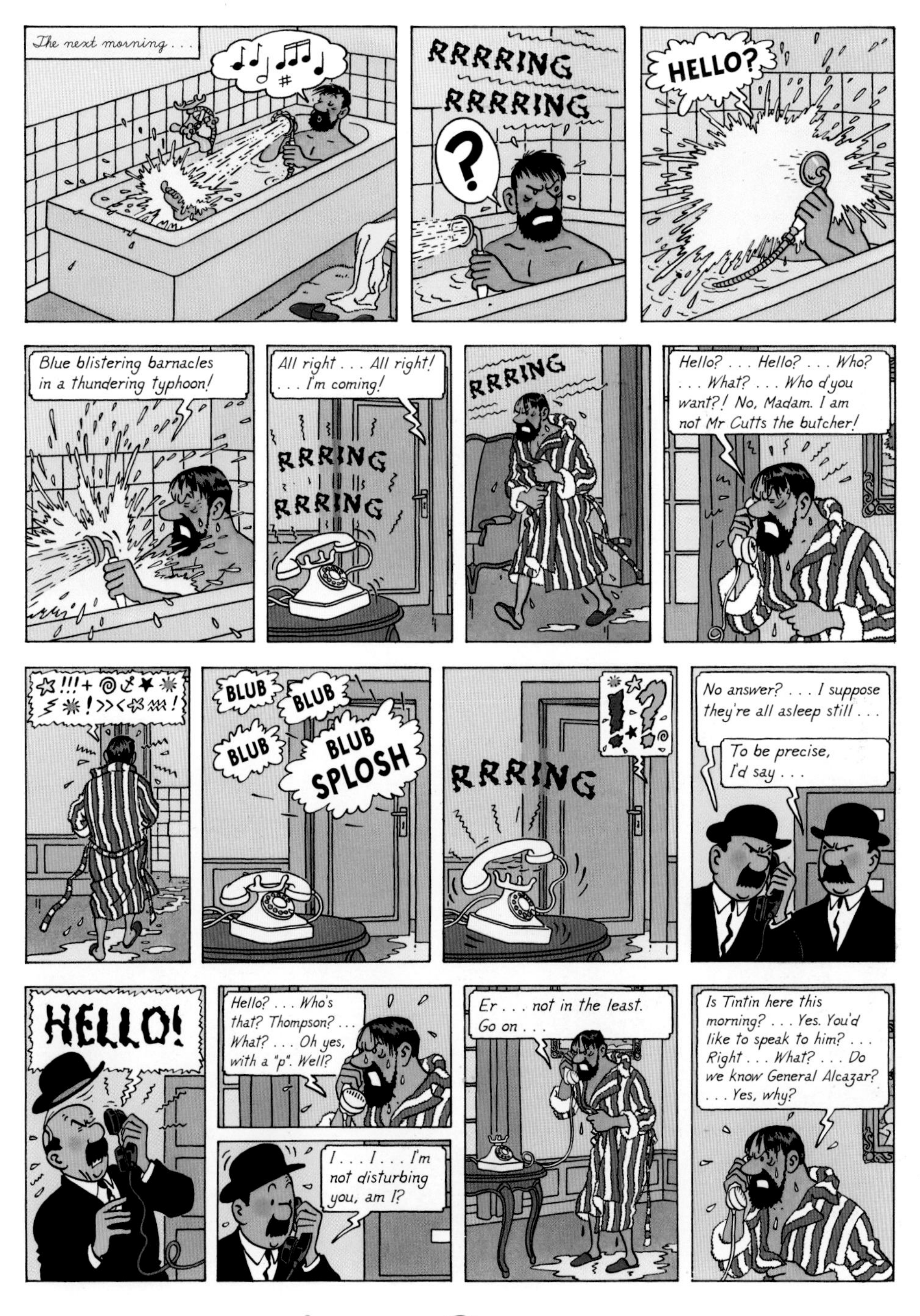
The next morning . . .
RRRRING
RRRRING
HELLO?
Blue blistering barnacles in a thundering typhoon!
All right . . . All right! . . . I'm coming!
RRRING
RRRING
RRRING
Hello? . . . Hello? . . . Who? . . . What? . . . Who d'you want?! No, Madam. I am not Mr Cutts the butcher!
BLUB
BLUB
BLUB
BLUB
SPLOSH
RRRING
No answer? . . . I suppose they're all asleep still . . .
To be precise, I'd say . . .
HELLO!
Hello? . . . Who's that? Thompson? . . . What? . . . Oh yes, with a "p". Well?
I . . . I . . . I'm not disturbing you, am I?
Er . . . not in the least. Go on . . .
Is Tintin here this morning? . . . Yes. You'd like to speak to him? . . . Right . . . What? . . . Do we know General Alcazar? . . . Yes, why?

You'll explain that to Tintin later? Good . . . What? . . . No, no trouble at all . . .
Ringing up when I'm in the bath! I ask you!
Half an hour later . . .
Well, well! Thompson and Thomson? . . . And they want to talk to me about General Alcazar. Odd, isn't it?
Yes . . . Talking of odd things . . . where's Abdullah this morning?
KHRRR KHRRR
?
Blistering barnacles, here he comes!
No, it's Calculus!
Good gracious!
You goat, you! D'you often feel impelled to come to breakfast on roller-skates?
Very well, thanks. And you?
Now admit it. You're puzzled to see me come in like that . . . Yes, yes, you find it odd, don't deny it! . . . Well, I can't tell you anything more at present . . .
RRRRING
?
. . . but quite soon you'll see my reason for it.
The Thompsons? Already! . . .
Ah! . . . Now for some breakfast.
D'you think so?

RRRRING
BANG
You thundering nitwitted numbskull you! Haven't you finished acting the goat yet?
Who rang, Nestor?
I found no one the first time, sir. But the second time, I saw Abdullah running away.
RRRING
I bet that's him! But he won't get away with it this time. Nestor, go and bring the hose-pipe!
Now . . . as soon as he rings, you open the door, and then: psshhtt! . . . We'll get a good laugh!
RRING
That's it! . . . Quick, open up, Nestor!
I . . . I'm dreadfully sorry! . . . Please forgive me! You see, it's Abdullah's fault. The young rapscallion kept ringing the bell . . .
Ha! ha! ha! ha!
?
A few minutes later . . .
Well, here's the position. Interpol have asked us to keep an eye on a man called Dawson, and to collect all the information we can about his activities . . .
. . . and also about the people he meets. It so happens that you know one of them: General Alcazar. What can you tell us about him?
Very little, as a matter of fact.
I knew him when he was President of the Republic of San Theodoros. I met him later, in Europe. He'd been deposed by his rival, General Tapioca, and had fled from his country. He'd become a knife-thrower on the music-halls . . . That's all.
All? Really? And what did he say to you, when you met him last night?
?

Aha! That surprised you, eh? You forget, my friend, in our job there's nothing we don't know.
To be precise: we know nothing in our job!
It's true that we met him last night. I was going to tell you . . . He said he was travelling, he was in a hurry, and he was staying at the Hotel . . . er . . . the Hotel . . .
Excelsior; yes, we know.
Oh? Well, that's the lot . . . He didn't say anything else . . . But what have you against him? What do you suspect?
Why are we suspect? I mean, what do we suspect? My dear fellow, if you imagine we'll tell you he's smuggling aircraft, you're much mistaken. "Mum's the word", that's our motto.
Well said! . . . To be precise: "Dumb's the word", that's our motto. The general may have come to Europe to buy up old aircraft, but you won't learn that from us! Now we must be going. Goodbye, Tintin.
Goodbye.
Ah! Here comes Nestor with our hats and sticks.
What a very peculiar thing: my hat has shrunk.
How strange. With me it's the opposite; I've got a swollen head . . .
Oh, I see. We've got muddled up. You have my hat and I have yours.
That's it: our mats are in a huddle. In short, we're contrarywise . . .
But it still isn't right!
Nor is mine!
May I see? . . . You can bet Abdullah's behind this . . .
Abdullalah?
There! . . . I thought as much. It's an old joke: newspapers folded up and slipped into the band.
A little later on . . .
Abdullah and his tricks!
Well, what did our Siamese twins want?
?

Just read this advertisement I've found in an old newspaper!
FOR SALE
AIRCRAFT, TANKS, SUBMARINES ETC
Further particulars from J.D.M.C., Box No. 5083, DR
EXPORT CO. LTD
Extraordinary! . . . Why don't they add: "on easy terms". You'll see, we'll end up buying a battleship or the 'Queen Mary' on the never-never!
Maybe. But did you notice the initials?
J.D.M.C. . . . J.D.M.C. . . . Thundering typhoons! Alcazar's wallet! The signature on that letter!
Precisely!
No doubt about it: the general's here to buy armaments. But that's no reason for failing to return his wallet. And since Thompson and Thomson have kindly told us the right address . . .
I'll come with you.
Later, at the Hotel Excelsior . . .
General Alcazar? Yes, he's here, sir. I just saw him go past. You'll find him in the lounge.
Thank you.
There . . .
Look . . . he's talking to someone. But . . . good heavens! It's Dawson. I've met him before. He was police chief in the International Settlement in Shanghai.
And there in the background, lurking behind their newspapers . . .
The Thompsons!
This all looks pretty fishy; I'd like to know a bit more about it. Listen, Captain; you stay here, and as soon as Dawson goes, you return General Alcazar's wallet. I'll follow Dawson. We'll meet at Marlinspike.
OK
An hour later . . .
There he is . . . getting into that black Jaguar.
EXCELSIOR
Quick, taxi! . . . Follow that black Jaguar, there, ahead of us.
Where are we off to now?

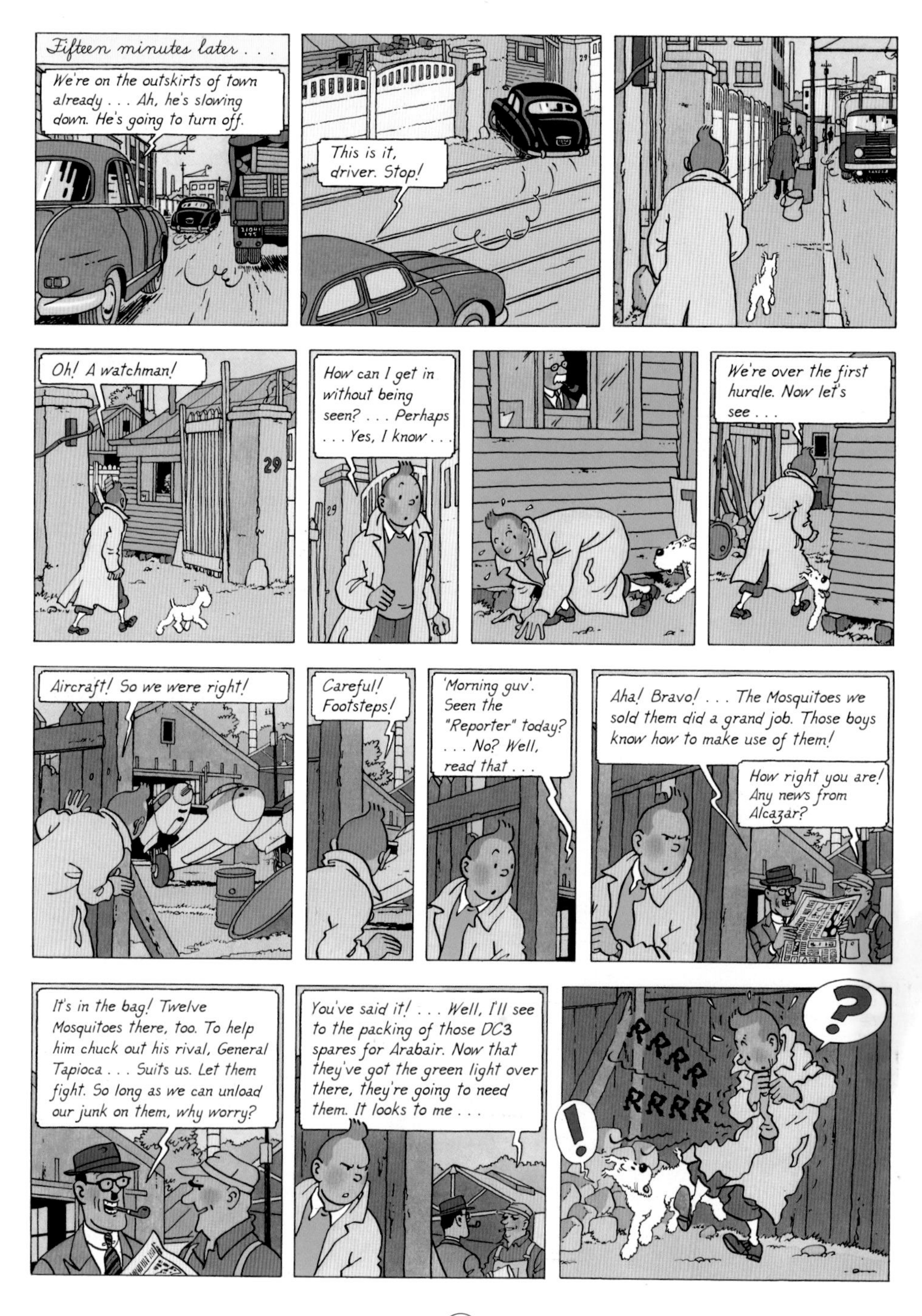
Fifteen minutes later . . .
We're on the outskirts of town already . . . Ah, he's slowing down. He's going to turn off.
This is it, driver. Stop!
Oh! A watchman!
How can I get in without being seen? . . . Perhaps . . . Yes, I know . . .
We're over the first hurdle. Now let's see . . .
Aircraft! So we were right!
Careful! Footsteps!
'Morning guv'. Seen the "Reporter" today? . . . No? Well, read that . . .
Aha! Bravo! . . . The Mosquitoes we sold them did a grand job. Those boys know how to make use of them!
How right you are! Any news from Alcazar?
It's in the bag! Twelve Mosquitoes there, too. To help him chuck out his rival, General Tapioca . . . Suits us. Let them fight. So long as we can unload our junk on them, why worry?
You've said it! . . . Well, I'll see to the packing of those DC3 spares for Arabair. Now that they've got the green light over there, they're going to need them. It looks to me . . .
RRRR RRRR
?
!

What's that? . . . What on earth's going on? . . . What's this confounded thing?
RRR RRR RRR
RRRR
Where the devil's that row coming from?!
RRR RRR
An alarm-clock!
!
RRRR RRRR
Abdullah, the little pest! I'll bet he put that alarm-clock in my pocket!
A young lad with a white dog, you say? . . . How did they manage to get in without your seeing?
"Daily Reporter" sir . . .
Thanks.
GASOLIN
CRUMBS!
Great Scot! What will the Captain think of this?
A little later . . .

Abdullah! Just you wait till I catch you!
Ha! ha! ha! ha!
Poor kid, all the same. He's too young to realise how serious things are.
BANG
?!
Blue blistering barnacles! This time I've had enough! . . . The little pest! A firework under my chair while I was having forty winks. It's the end! He's going back to his father!
Too late! . . . Read this . . .
COUP D'ÉTAT IN KHEMED
Wadesdah in Rebel Hands
AIR POWER ENSURES REBEL VICTORY
Aircraft Riddle: Who supplied the Mosquitoes?
Bab El Ehr has seized power.
Emir Ben Ka prisoner of
Special Correspondent in Beirut.
Thundering typhoons! The poor Emir! This explains the serious situation he mentioned in his letter . . . Well, you're right: we can't send Abdullah home.
No, but . . .
. . . perhaps there's another way out. If we can't send him off, there's nothing to stop us going away ourselves.
Tintin, you're a genius. But . . . where can we go?
Where? . . . Well, what about Khemed?
That's it! Khemed . . . Good idea!
What? Khemed? In the middle of a revolution! You're crazy! . . . What could we do there?
Perhaps we might try to rescue the Emir. At the same time, we could try to clear up this odd business of the aircraft.
No, thanks, not for me! . . . You go if you like . . . I'm staying here!
BANG
All right, I'm coming.

A youngster with a white dog? That reminds me of something . . . but what?
RRRING RRRING
Hello? . . . Who's that? . . . Oh, it's you, General . . . What? . . . Oh, your wallet . . . You've got it back?
Yes, they bring him back. This Captain Haddock, who I meet yesterday with one of my friends . . . Tintin . . . Qué? . . . Si, Tintin. You know him? . . . Qué? The telephone call you receive last night? . . . Yes, it was him. He find your number in my wallet.
Tintin! . . . So he's the one sticking his nose into my business! . . . I'll soon take care of him . . .
The airport at Wadesdah, capital of Khemed, three days later . . .
Here comes the plane from Beirut.
You understand? If he's aboard, you put this briefcase in the baggage compartment.
WADESDAH AIRPORT
I'm not sorry to get here . . . With these old crates you can never be sure . . .
I say, have you noticed? . . . Armed men all over the place.
Passports, please gentlemen.
I am sorry, gentlemen: you have no permit to stay in Khemed. You must reboard the plane, and return to Beirut.

Blistering barnacles! What sort of a yarn is that?
Here are your passports. You will be conducted to the aircraft.
Thundering typhoons! You're not getting away with this! Our passports are perfectly in order . . . You have no right . . .
Billions of blistering barnacles! To have come so far, and then be held up by these Bashi-bazouks! It's absolutely infuriating!
An hour later . . .
There they go! In an hour they'll be flying over the mountains . . . Jebel Kadheh . . . Then . . .
Another eternity in this flying coffin! . . . And a bumpy trip into the bargain. Rattled about like dice in a box . . . I just wonder what sort of trouble will drop on us next.
Thundering typhoons! Why does everything happen to me?
Look out, Captain!
Another . . .
. . . air-pocket!
You're not hurt, are you?
Not at all. I'm just enjoying the luxurious comfort of air travel!
TICK
TOCK
TICK
TOCK
TICK
TOCK

Golly! I can smell trouble. There's something sinister going on here. I must warn Tintin at once.
KH-OZD
I'm wondering WHO warned the authorities at Wadesdah of our arrival, and WHO persuaded them to deport us?
Hello, Snowy, what's the matter?
WOOAH! WOOAH!
Here, will you stop that! You know, he . . . yes, he wants to show me something. All right, I'll follow you . . .
WOOAH! WOOAH!
In there? It's the luggage. You want me to go in? All right, I'm coming.
WOOAH! WOOAH!
PH-E-E-E-T
?
PH-E-E-E-T
What's that siren for?
الخربيقو
An engine on fire! That's the alarm for the extinguishers!
OZD
Thundering typhoons! The extinguishers haven't worked; it's burning more fiercely than ever!
Wadesdah Tower . . . Wadesdah Tower . . . This is KH-OZD . . . Starboard motor on fire . . . Extinguishers unserviceable. We're turning back . . . We'll try to reach Wadesdah.
It's no good! It's too heavy. I shall just have to . . .
TOCK
TICK
TICK
TOCK
TICK TOCK

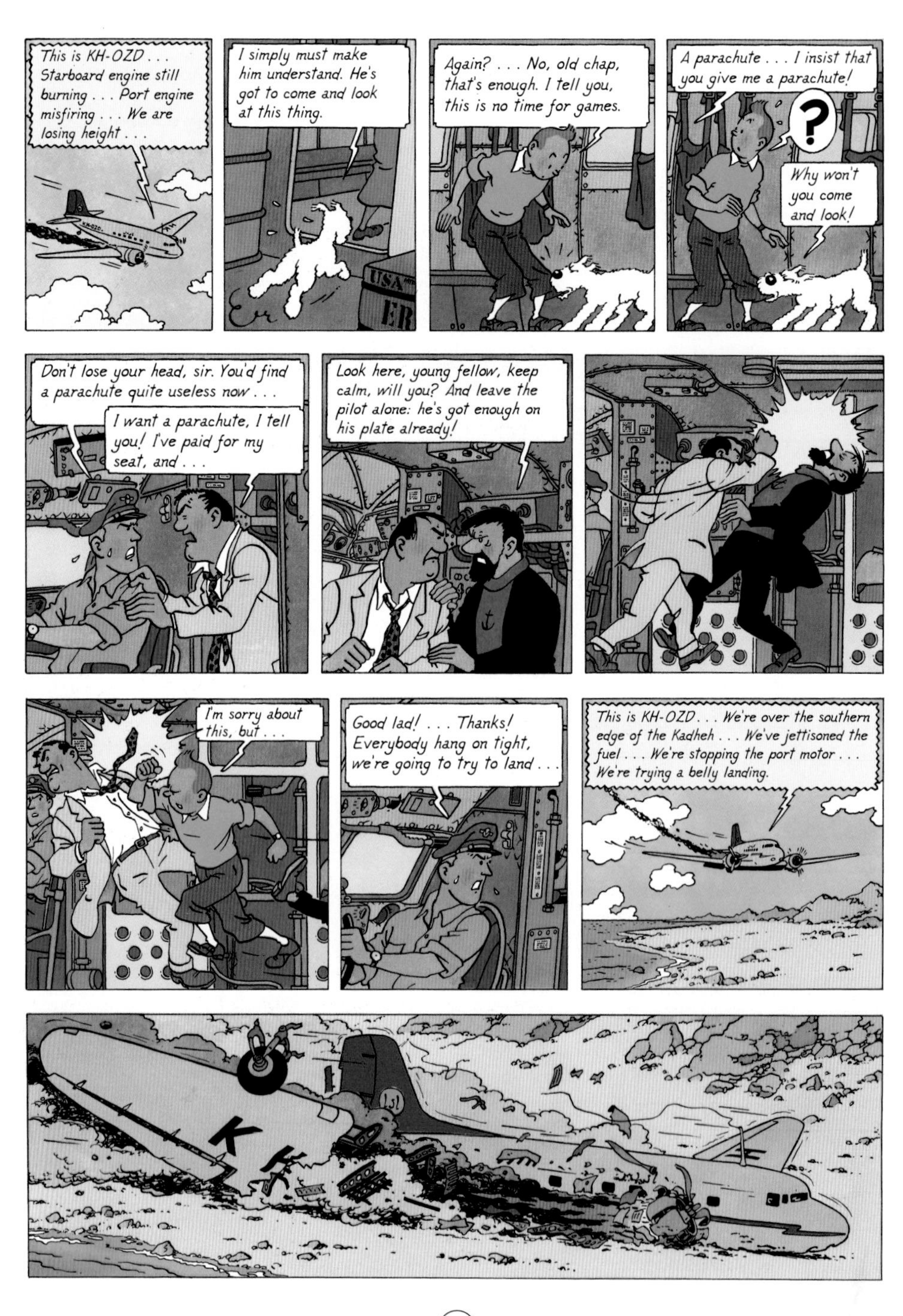

This is KH-OZD . . . Starboard engine still burning . . . Port engine misfiring . . . We are losing height . . .
I simply must make him understand. He's got to come and look at this thing.
Again? . . . No, old chap, that's enough. I tell you, this is no time for games.
A parachute . . . I insist that you give me a parachute!
?
Why won't you come and look!
Don't lose your head, sir. You'd find a parachute quite useless now . . .
I want a parachute, I tell you! I've paid for my seat, and . . .
Look here, young fellow, keep calm, will you? And leave the pilot alone: he's got enough on his plate already!
I'm sorry about this, but . . .
Good lad! . . . Thanks! Everybody hang on tight, we're going to try to land . . .
This is KH-OZD . . . We're over the southern edge of the Kadheh . . . We've jettisoned the fuel . . . We're stopping the port motor . . . We're trying a belly landing.

Allah be praised! . . . We are safe!
Whew! that's it! The fire is out.
Don't stay here in the open sun. We'd better move into the shadow of those rocks, while we wait for a rescue party.
Come out of there, Snowy! At once!
Wooah! Wooah!
Wooah! Wooah!
No, no, there's no need to worry. Wadesdah was alerted, and it's only thirty miles away. They'll soon be out looking for us.
?
A few minutes later . . .
I say, Captain, if we stay here they'll take us back to Wadesdah, and we'll be expelled once again . . . Wait a minute, Snowy . . . It seems to be about thirty miles to the city. Suppose we make ourselves scarce . . .
Wooah! Wooah!
On foot?
Yes, on foot . . . I'm just going back to the plane. Snowy's incorrigible; he absolutely insists on showing me something.
So you're coming at last!
All right, Snowy . . . I'm coming with you.
Thirty miles! A mere trifle!
Thirty miles . . . And I've still got . . . Let's see . . . I've still got . . .
. . . half a bottle of whisky . . . that's 240 miles to the gallon . . . not too good, but still . . .
BOOM

My bottle! . . . I must save my bottle!
Thundering typhoons! The plane's blown up!
But my bottle's safe!
Columbus! . . . Tintin?
He went towards the plane . . . Let's hope . . . Careful: mustn't break my bottle . . .
TINTIN! . . . TINTIN! . . .
SMASH
Billions of blistering barnacles!
Tintin, old man! . . . You aren't broken? . . . I mean . . . you aren't hurt?
N . . . no. I was just knocked flat by the blast. But Snowy? Where's Snowy?
Safe and sound. He's fetching your hat.
Snowy, good old Snowy. You scented danger, eh? . . . And I just thought you wanted to play.
You know, Tintin, you ought to take me more seriously.
A time-bomb in the baggage compartment . . . So it's thanks to the fire in the starboard motor that we're still alive! . . . Normally, at this time, we'd be flying over the mountains, over the Jebel . . . You can imagine, if we'd blown up in the air . . .
Yes, we've had a lucky escape. I wonder . . .
What?
Nothing . . . but I think we won't hang around here. Let's go.
All right. I agree.

When we get to Wadesdah, we'll seek shelter with our old friend Senhor Oliveira de Figueira.
SNIFF SNIFF
We mustn't run into the rescue party on the way . . . As soon as our disappearance is reported, they'll start searching for us.
WOOAAH . . .
YOW . . .
YEOW . . .
Night has fallen . . .
I've had enough of this little jaunt! . . . If we go on much longer I'll be on my knees! If only I could lie down!
Lie down? We simply must reach Wadesdah before dawn, Captain. Lying down is out of the question.
Quick, lie down!
Make up your mind . . . shall I lie down, or not?
A patrol! I'm sure they're out looking for us.
Halt! . . . Who goes there?
I heard a noise . . . a sort of rumbling . . .
It's just an aeroplane . . . Listen.
For heaven's sake stop snoring!
Me, snoring? I didn't hear anything.
Whew! . . . They've gone.
Oh, good . . . ZZZ . . .
Come on, Captain, get up. We're moving on.
I'll have my breakfast in bed, Nestor . . . ZZZ . . . ZZZ . . .
It isn't Nestor, Captain, it's Tintin! . . . Get up, hurry!
ZZZ
What on earth can I do? Let's hope they don't come back . . .
ZZZ . . . ZZZ . . . ZZZ . . .

I always keep a small flask of rum for emergencies. Now's the time to use it . . .
This confounded cork won't come out . . .
Ah! . . . That's it!
POP
POP = = = WHISKY
Aaah! Now then, where are those sprouts? . . . I mean scouts . . . ? I'd l-l-like a word or two w-w-with them!
Stop! That's enough!
Sh! Be quiet! We must get on.
Early next day . . .
Wadesdah at last! Now we must be careful . . . The main gates will be watched; but I know a small gateway, and that'll be unguarded.
There, you see. We got in unmolested. Now we must find Senhor Oliveira de Figueira. I'm sure his house is near here.
Yes, that's it. I remember.
You did say he always has a bottle of wine handy?
Senhor Oliveira! . . . Senhor Oliveira! . . .
The joke's on us if he's moved!
Senhor Oliveira! . . . Senhor Oliveira! . . . Open the door! It's Tintin!
?
Blistering barnacles! . . . A patrol!
Quick, we must find somewhere to hide!
Who's that?

Patrol . . . Who's that? . . .
What do you mean: who's that? I'm asking you! . . . What's the idea, waking people up at this hour?
We can't help it if you're a light sleeper!
A light sleeper! . . . What a nerve! After all the row you've been making!
Well, never mind! . . . Next time we'll walk on our hands, to save waking the most noble Dom Oliveira!
I . . . oh, go to the devil!
Just listen to that! There's one we haven't woken up, anyway! . . . What a din! . . . Ha! ha! ha! ha!
He! he! he!
Ho! ho! ho!
ZZZ ZZZ
Whew! They've gone! That gave me a fright! Come on, Captain, stop snoring for goodness sake!
REWARD
TINTIN
HADDOCK
ZZZ ZZZ ZZZ
RAT TAT TAT
Again!!!
By the beard of your Prophet, will you go away and let me sleep!
Open the door, Senhor Oliveira! It's Tintin! Please open up!
Tintin! . . . You here! . . . Come in quickly . . . quickly!
ZZZ ZZZ ZZZ
What are you doing here? Don't you know there's a price on your head?
I know . . . I've just seen the poster.
Goodnight, everybody.
It's incredible! . . . Fantastic! . . . I can't believe it! . . . But first of all: I'm sure you must be hungry? . . .
Rather . . .
ZZZ ZZZ
Thirsty, too?
Er . . . a drop of your wine would save our lives.
Now then, tell me what you're doing in Khemed.
It's like this . . .
. . . and so Abdullah . . .
. . . aircraft for sale . . .
. . . letter from the Emir . . .
. . . flew to Wadesdah . . .
. . . Then we decided to set out for Wadesdah on foot, and to come to you . . .
It was wise of you. Now, I'll bring you up to date on the situation in Khemed. Six months ago . . .
ZZZ ZZZ ZZZ
ACTION STATIONS!
?!

I . . . What was that? . . . Er . . . forgive me . . . I . . . I think I was dreaming . . . A nightmare . . . Pirates . . .
Oh, well . . .
I'll light up. That'll help me to stay awake.
Good idea.
Where was I? . . . Oh yes . . . I was saying that six months ago, as a result of an agreement between the Emir and Arabair, Wadesdah became an important link in the air route to Mecca. Then, a few weeks ago, it seems that trouble blew up between Arabair and the Emir. The situation began to deteriorate . . .
. . . As if by chance, trouble flared up all over the country, and Sheik Bab El Ehr took command of the rebels. These rebels were supported by a powerful air force which, so to speak, came out of the blue. The rebels marched on Wadesdah, and seized power.
It all puzzles me, Senhor Oliveira. You see, the rebel Mosquitoes and the Arabair DC3's came from the same source . . . And I'd like to know what touched off the dispute between the Emir and Arabair.
Er . . . I've no idea at all.
Oh? . . . Well . . . We'll go into that later. The most urgent thing is to help the Emir. What's become of him?
He had to flee. He took refuge in the Jebel with Patrash Pasha, whose fierce tribesmen remained loyal.
HAAAAH! . . .
!
What . . . what . . . what . . . what happened?
Your pipe, Captain. It set fire to your beard.
Come, it's time for sleep. Tomorrow we will find some way for you to leave the city, and join the Emir.
Yes. Good.
Two days later . . .
D'you see, there? . . . A patrol coming . . .
I know . . . Keep calm!
TEN THOU . . .
?

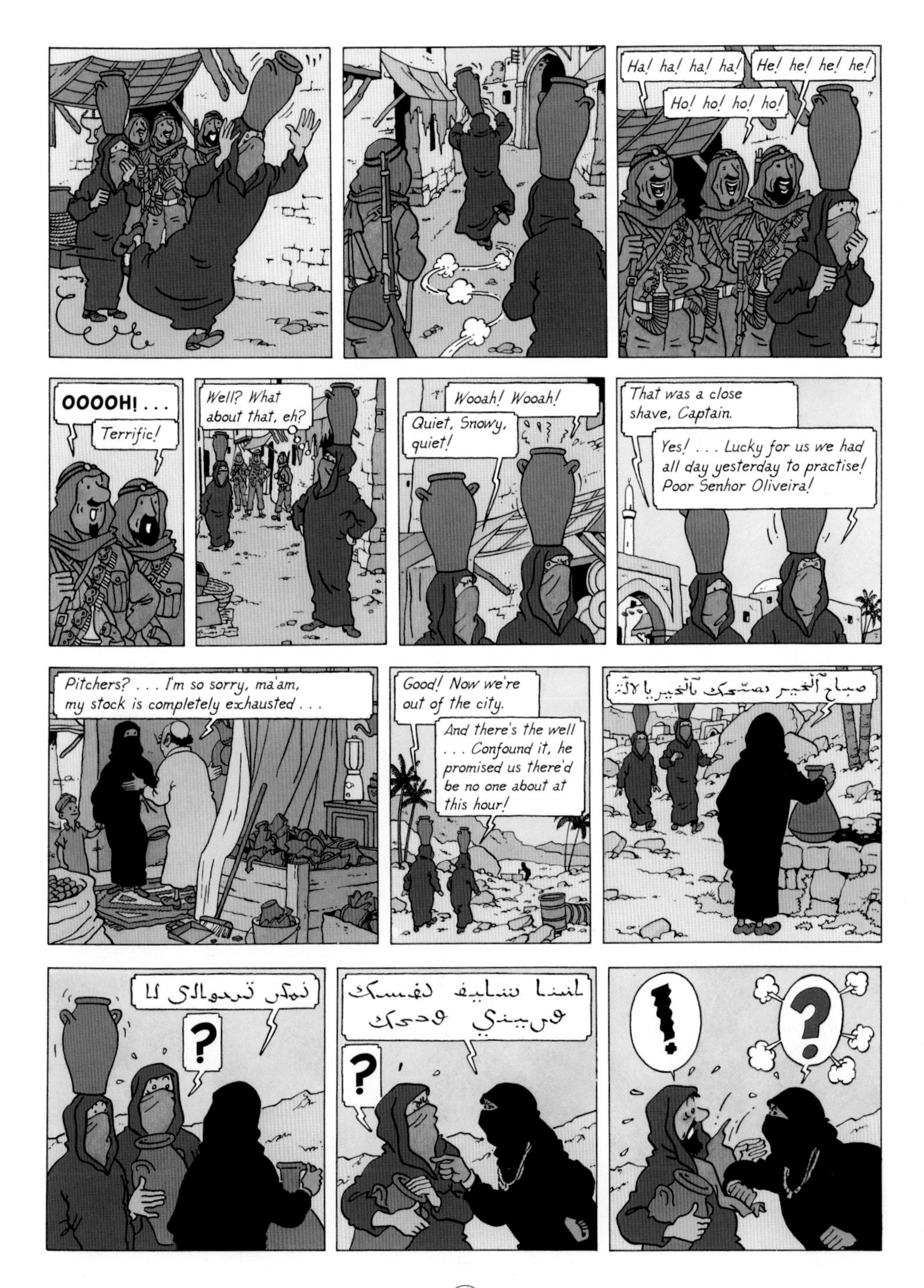

Ha! ha! ha! ha!
He! he! he! he!
Ho! ho! ho! ho!
OOOOH! . . .
Terrific!
Well? What about that, eh?
Wooah! Wooah!
Quiet, Snowy, quiet!
That was a close shave, Captain.
Yes! . . . Lucky for us we had all day yesterday to practise! Poor Senhor Oliveira!
Pitchers? . . . I'm so sorry, ma'am, my stock is completely exhausted . . .
Good! Now we're out of the city.
And there's the well . . . Confound it, he promised us there'd be no one about at this hour!
?
?
!
?

Why can't you talk English like everyone else, you fancy-dress Fatima?! What do you want, anyway?
WOOAH!
Billions of blue blistering barnacles! That old witch will raise the alarm! . . .
. . . And our guide isn't here! . . . Oliveira was quite definite that he'd wait near the well, with the horses . . . Now what is it, Snowy?
Wooah! . . . Wooah! . . .
There he is! Fine! Back in the saddle again . . .
And a few minutes later . . .
My stirrups, blistering barnacles! . . . My stirrups! . . .
Meanwhile . . .
Hello, Colonel Achmed? . . . This is Mull Pasha at Sheik Bab El Ehr's headquarters . . . Order your Mosquitoes to take off immediately . . . Hello? . . . Yes. Their mission: to wipe out a party of three horsemen who have left Wadesdah, heading for the Jebel . . . You understand? . . . Good . . . Armoured cars are already on the way . . . Hello? . . . Yes, they are partisans of Ben Kalish Ezab . . . Yes, wipe them out.
There they are! . . . Fire!

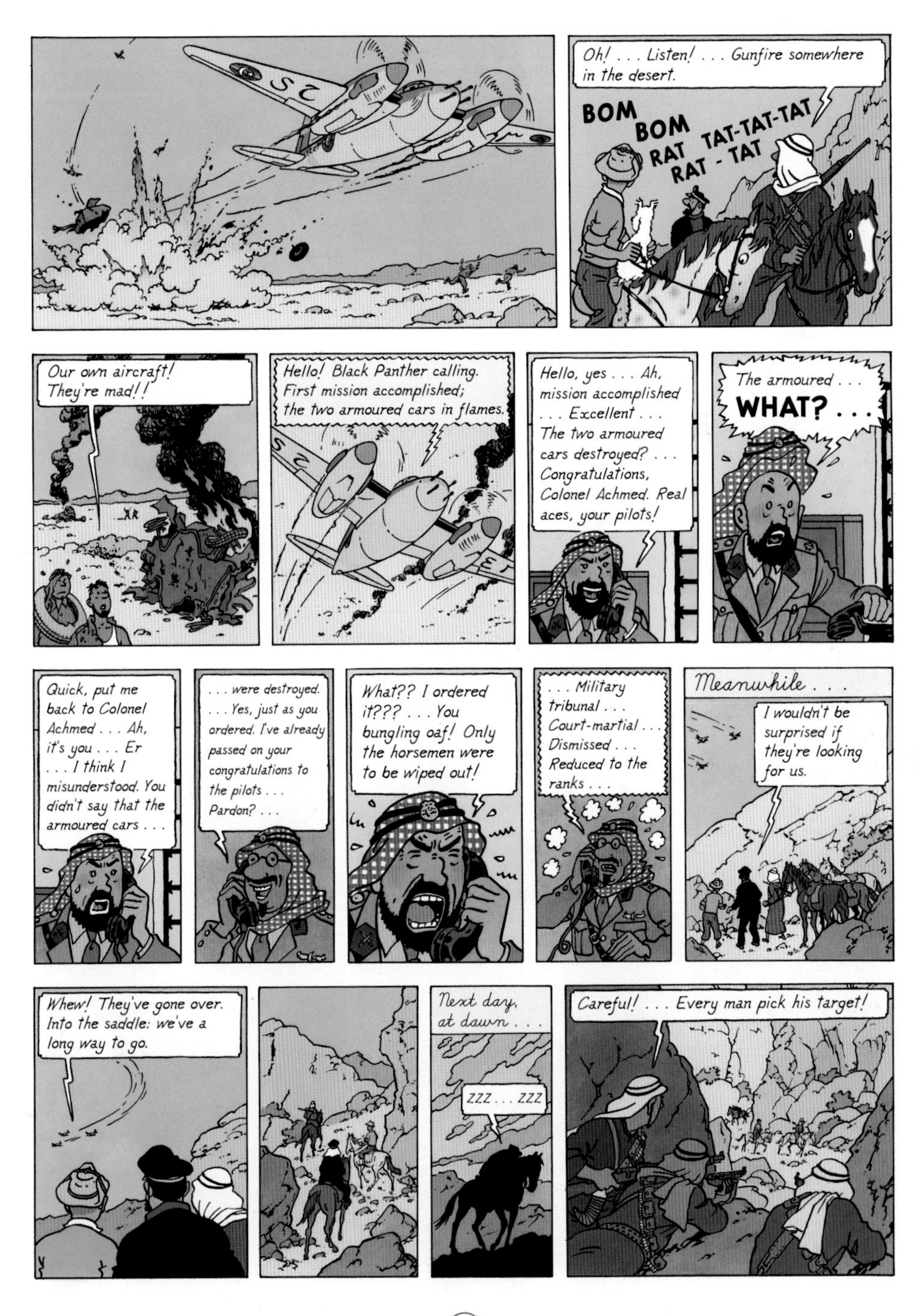
Oh! . . . Listen! . . . Gunfire somewhere in the desert.
BOM BOM RAT TAT-TAT-TAT RAT - TAT
Our own aircraft! They're mad!!
Hello! Black Panther calling. First mission accomplished; the two armoured cars in flames.
Hello, yes . . . Ah, mission accomplished . . . Excellent . . . The two armoured cars destroyed? . . . Congratulations, Colonel Achmed. Real aces, your pilots!
The armoured . . . WHAT? . . .
Quick, put me back to Colonel Achmed . . . Ah, it's you . . . Er . . . I think I misunderstood. You didn't say that the armoured cars . . .
. . . were destroyed. . . . Yes, just as you ordered. I've already passed on your congratulations to the pilots . . . Pardon? . . .
What?? I ordered it??? . . . You bungling oaf! Only the horsemen were to be wiped out!
. . . Military tribunal . . . Court-martial . . . Dismissed . . . Reduced to the ranks . . .
Meanwhile . . .
I wouldn't be surprised if they're looking for us.
Whew! They've gone over. Into the saddle: we've a long way to go.
Next day, at dawn . . .
ZZZ . . . ZZZ
Careful! . . . Every man pick his target!

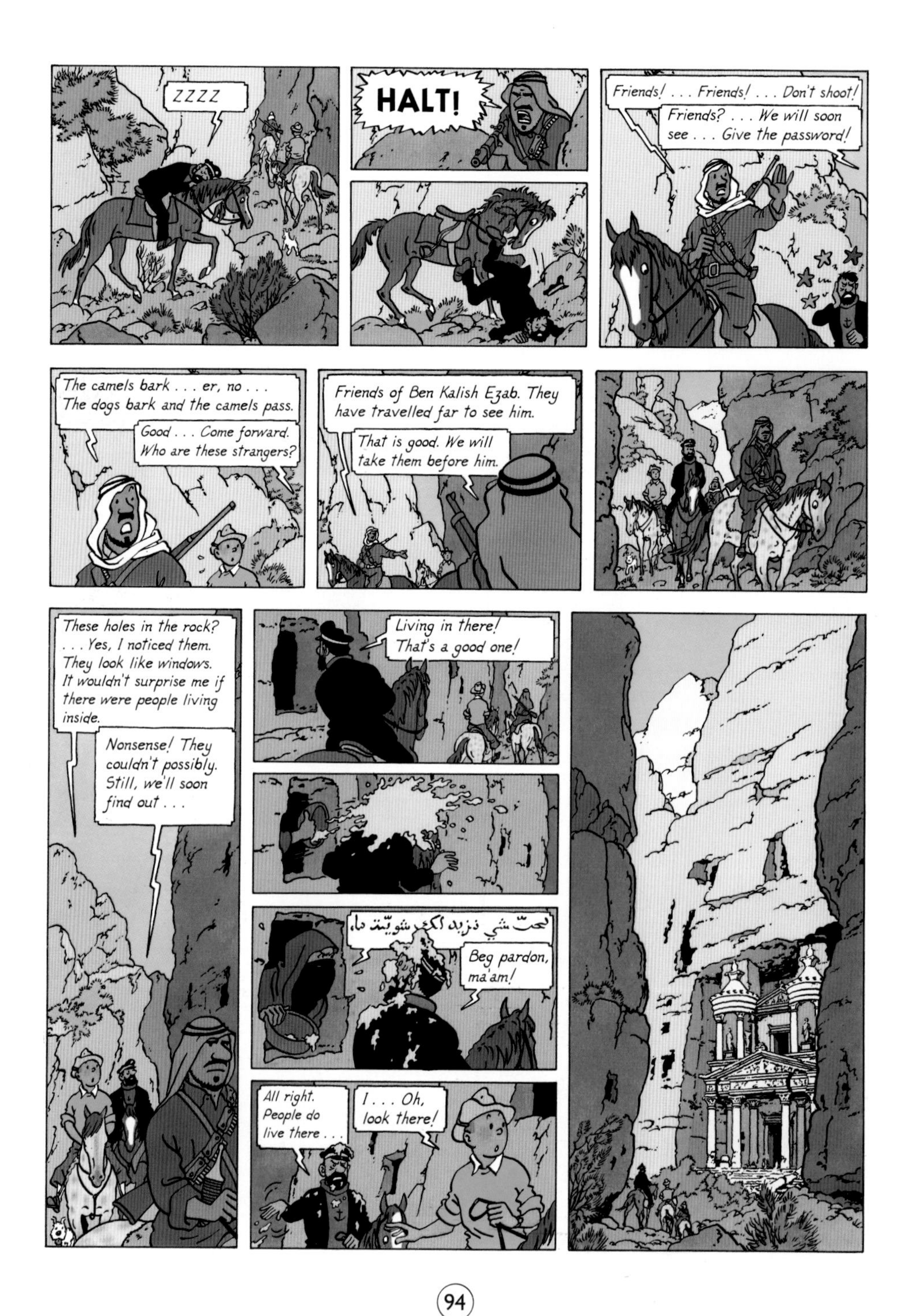
ZZZZ
HALT!
Friends! . . . Friends! . . . Don't shoot!
Friends? . . . We will soon see . . . Give the password!
The camels bark . . . er, no . . . The dogs bark and the camels pass.
Good . . . Come forward. Who are these strangers?
Friends of Ben Kalish Ezab. They have travelled far to see him.
That is good. We will take them before him.
These holes in the rock? . . . Yes, I noticed them. They look like windows. It wouldn't surprise me if there were people living inside.
Nonsense! They couldn't possibly. Still, we'll soon find out . . .
Living in there! That's a good one!
Beg pardon, ma'am!
All right. People do live there . . .
I . . . Oh, look there!

Thundering typhoons! . . . A Roman temple, hewn from the rock! . . . Incredible!
We have arrived.
A few minutes later . . .
How stupendous! An entire city carved out of the mountain.
Tintin! . . . Captain! . . . You here? . . . It is unbelievable!
And my son? . . . My own little treasure? My precious darling . . . Where is he?
Ah, yes . . . We left him at Marlinspike, Your Highness. But rest assured, he is in good hands.
Poor little lamb! How sad he must be, so far from his Papa.
And now I'll leave you tied to the palm tree, so the crocodiles can come and eat you. Ha! ha! We're having fun, aren't we, Nestor? . . .
Confounded brat! . . . Ah, someone's coming. They'll set me free.
Ah, Nestor, I was looking for you. Could you give me a hand? It's nothing much: simply give me a little push.
Mmmm! . . . Mmm!
It's to test the new steering mechanism I've fitted to my roller-skates . . . Quite simple, really. They use the same principle for steering model cars.
Mmm! . . . Mm!
For instance, at the moment, my skates are locked right over to the left . . . If someone were to push me now I should turn round more or less on the same spot.
Mmm! . . . Mmm!
But I'm quite sure that despite his sadness my cherub is a little ray of sunshine, bringing life and gaiety into your old home.
Undoubtedly!

And you, what brings you here? . . . Come along in and sit down. You must be tired. And you'll certainly be hungry and thirsty. I will have some refreshments brought to you.
Well, Your Highness, we are here to try and help you; also, to get to the bottom of a mystery, in which Arabair seem to have an important part.
Arabair? The dogs! . . . They will pay dearly for their treachery . . . I gave them permission to establish a base at Wadesdah, an important link on the route to Mecca . . .
One day, about three months ago, my little Abdullah, my flawless jewel, expressed a wish to see the Arabair planes loop the loop a few times before landing at Wadesdah . . .
Loop the loop!? But,, Highness . . .
Nothing simpler, don't you agree? . . . And it would have given my lambkin such pleasure! . . . Well, instead of seizing this opportunity of pleasing my little sugar-plum, they refused, on some trumped-up excuse . . .
But Highness . . .
Naturally, I was very angry and threatened to terminate our agreement. I also used another threat: that I would reveal to the world that Arabair are involved in slave trading.
WHAT?. . .
?
GRRR . . .
Slave trading, no less . . . Their planes touching down at Wadesdah on the way from Africa are always full to bursting with native Sudanese and Senegalese. These are Mohammedan converts, making their pilgrimage to Mecca.
Yes, go on . . .
On the other hand, on the return journey their planes are mostly empty . . . Why? . . . Because somewhere between Wadesdah and Mecca these unfortunate negroes are sold as slaves.
But that's frightful!
Er . . . Yes . . . But to get back to Arabair: these jackals stirred up trouble in my country, and thanks to their support, the accursed Bab El Ehr was able to seize power . . . But it won't be for long . . . I'll throw him out, that mangy dog, that stinking hyena, that slimy serpent, that . . .
GRAOW
By Allah! . . . Let us hope your dog hasn't gone near Ayesha!
GRRAOW
?
!
?
CRACK
GRAOW

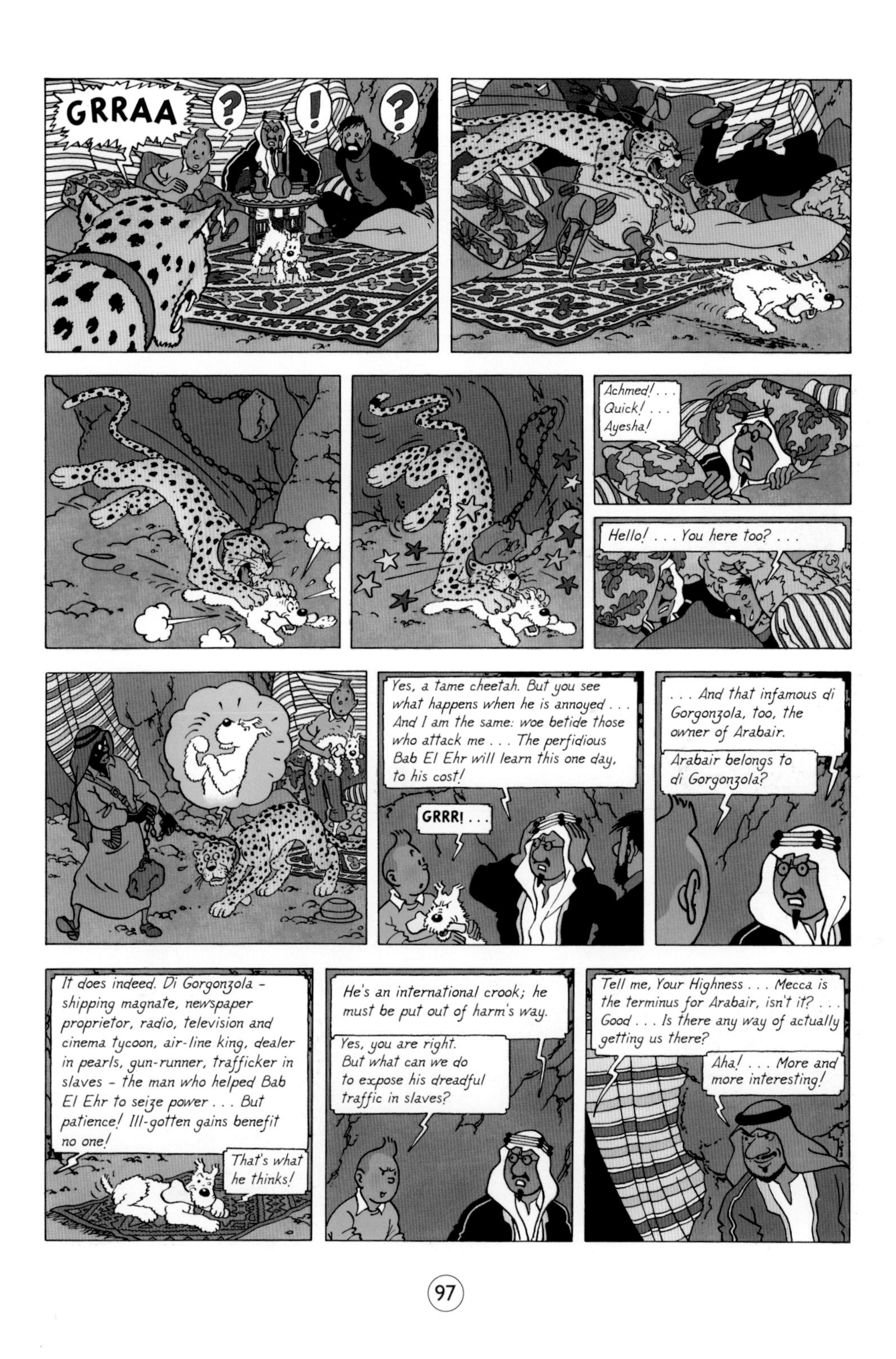
GRRAA
?
!
?
Achmed! . . .
Quick! . . .
Ayesha!
Hello! . . . You here too? . . .
Yes, a tame cheetah. But you see what happens when he is annoyed . . . And I am the same: woe betide those who attack me . . . The perfidious Bab El Ehr will learn this one day, to his cost!
GRRR! . . .
. . . And that infamous di Gorgonzola, too, the owner of Arabair.
Arabair belongs to di Gorgonzola?
It does indeed. Di Gorgonzola - shipping magnate, newspaper proprietor, radio, television and cinema tycoon, air-line king, dealer in pearls, gun-runner, trafficker in slaves - the man who helped Bab El Ehr to seize power . . . But patience! Ill-gotten gains benefit no one!
That's what he thinks!
He's an international crook; he must be put out of harm's way.
Yes, you are right. But what can we do to expose his dreadful traffic in slaves?
Tell me, Your Highness . . . Mecca is the terminus for Arabair, isn't it? . . . Good . . . Is there any way of actually getting us there?
Aha! . . . More and more interesting!

To Mecca? That's not easy at the moment. But if you will give me two or three days, I will find means of putting you aboard a sailing-ship, which will take you there.
Thank you, Highness.
Aha! This will please Bab El Ehr . . .
GRAOW!
Again? What has happened now?
It is Ben Yussef, O Master . . . Ayesha jumped on him . . . See, it will be at least three weeks before he is well . . . It seems that he trod on Ayesha's tail . . .
Oh, poor creature!
Three days later . . .
There, everything is arranged. You leave tomorrow at dawn, with two trusted men. They will lead you to a point on the coast where a small vessel will be waiting to take you to Mecca. But be on your guard. Di Gorgonzola is a dangerous man.
Two days have passed . . .
Here we are . . . You may dismount . . . But stay while I make sure that the boat has arrived.
He's signalling to us . . . We can go.
Ah, so that's the tub we're going to board. It's a dhow . . . No; I beg your pardon: a sambuk.
Look, they have just put a boat out.
Danger! Danger! A mounted patrol!

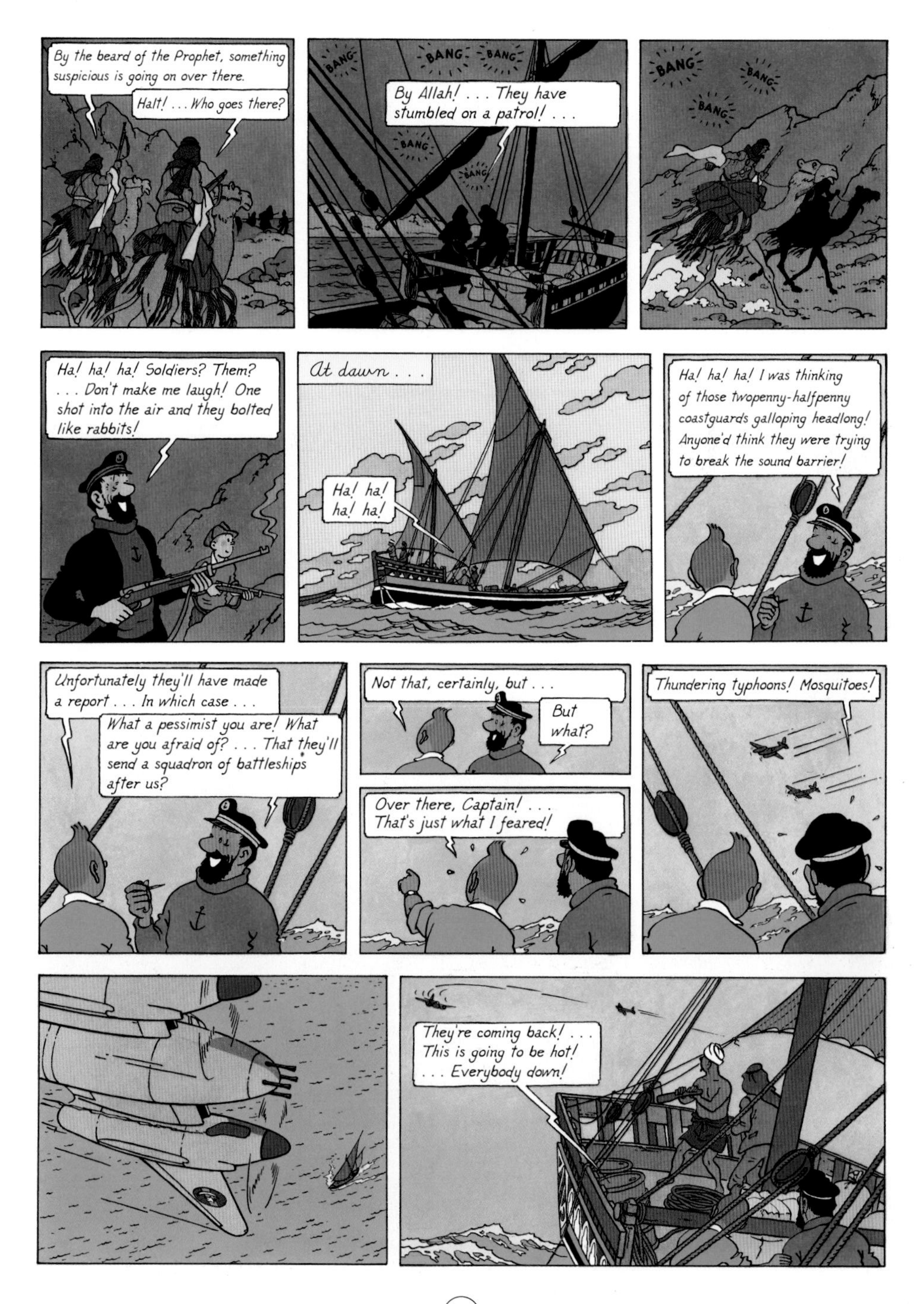
BANG BANG BANG BANG BANG
By the beard of the Prophet, something suspicious is going on over there.
Halt! ... Who goes there?
By Allah! . . . They have stumbled on a patrol! . . .
BANG BANG BANG
Ha! ha! ha! Soldiers? Them? . . . Don't make me laugh! One shot into the air and they bolted like rabbits!
At dawn . . .
Ha! ha! ha! ha!
Ha! ha! ha! I was thinking of those twopenny-halfpenny coastguards galloping headlong! Anyone'd think they were trying to break the sound barrier!
Unfortunately they'll have made a report . . . In which case . . .
What a pessimist you are! What are you afraid of? . . . That they'll send a squadron of battleships after us?
Not that, certainly, but . . .
But what?
Over there, Captain! . . . That's just what I feared!
Thundering typhoons! Mosquitoes!
They're coming back! . . . This is going to be hot! . . . Everybody down!

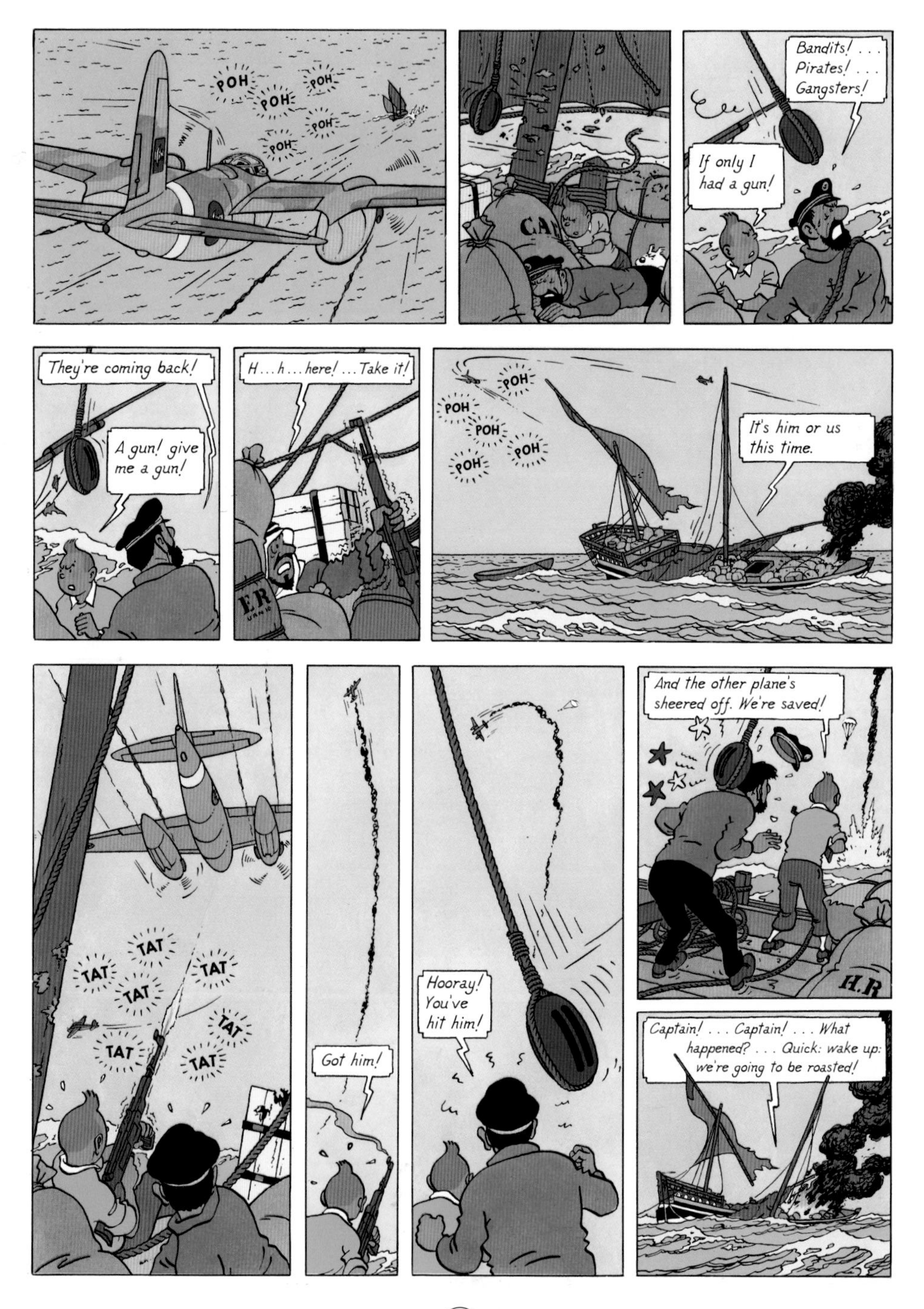
POH
POH
POH
POH
POH
Bandits! . . .
Pirates! . . .
Gangsters!
If only I had a gun!
They're coming back!
A gun! give me a gun!
H . . . h . . . here! . . . Take it!
POH
POH
POH
POH
POH
It's him or us this time.
TAT
TAT
TAT
TAT
TAT
TAT
TAT
Got him!
Hooray! You've hit him!
And the other plane's sheered off. We're saved!
Captain! . . . Captain! . . . What happened? . . . Quick: wake up: we're going to be roasted!

I don't know what happened . . . Some coward hit me from behind.
But who? . . . We're on our own. The crew have taken the boat and made off.
Quick, get down . . . That's what knocked you out!
Thundering typhoons! My nose!
So sorry . . . But there's no time to waste. We must build a raft, or we'll be grilled alive.
A quarter of an hour later . . .
Billions of blue blistering barnacles! . . . We've saved two cases of provisions, and no tin-opener; it's enough to drive you crazy!
What about trying with your knife?
Oh! There's the pilot from the plane we shot down!
Him!!! Let him take care of himself . . . Er . . . Is he far away?
No, quite near. Here, help me rescue him.
You've done a good job, eh? You trigger-happy thug! Who are you, anyway? What's your name?
Skut.
What do you mean, scoot? I'll teach you manners, you blithering bombardier. I'll soon deflate you! Ectoplasm!
But . . . but . . . my name Skut . . . Piotr Skut . . . Me Esthonian . . .
Look out! . . . Mind your knife!
BANG
Er . . . Oh! Skut . . . So your name's Skut, eh? . . . Er, I . . . Well, don't let it bother you!
Meanwhile . . .
Hello! hello! . . . This is R3KO . . . This is R3KO calling K6VM . . . Over.
Hello! Hello! This is K6VM . . . This is K6VM . . . Come in R3KO . . . Come in . . . Over.

Meanwhile . . .
May I have the pleasure of this samba, Princess?
But of course, Marquis.
What an ideal yacht for a cruise!
The "Scheherazade" is certainly a wonderful ship . . . And what a good idea to have a fancy-dress ball on board . . . Ma-a-arvellous!
Excuse me, my lord, there is a radio call for you . . . It's urgent . . .
Very well, I'm coming.
You see, dear lady? Business, always business. I am indeed a slave . . . Will you forgive me?
Don't give it a thought.
What an entrancing host he is. This cruise aboard the "Scheherazade" is really too enchanting!
Yes, he's a true gentleman. Naturally, malicious tongues spread rumours that he has a shady past . . .
It's only to be expected that such luxury arouses envy. One must admit . . .
Hello! Hello! K6VM calling R3KO . . . Transmit in code . . . Over.
Powerful insects have stung the blue goat. Parasites 1 and 2 are in the bag. Out.
K6VM to R3KO. Understood. Out.
Good . . . Now for the book, and we'll decode this. Parasites 1 and 2 - I know who they are!
There . . . I have it . . . Excellent! Mull Pasha has done well. We're rid of those two meddlers!
MOLIERE
If this goes on, Captain, we'll soon be on Dr Bombard's diet: plankton and sea-water.

Me? . . . Drink sea-water? . . .
Are you out of your mind?
Try some, Captain. It's not as bad as all that.
Ha! ha! ha! Not as bad as all that! . . . Think of all the dead fish there must be in it . . . All the people drowned in it over the centuries . . . All the tons of rubbish dumped from ships every day . . . You can commit suicide if you like, drinking that pig-swill. But for me it's "niet, niet", all along the line!
This not good . . .
Besides . . . Besides . . .
Besides . . . Besides . . .
YIPPEEE
?
There! . . . A ship! . . . Saved!
A ship . . . Just when you've swallowed that liquid manure! Ha! ha! ha! What a scream!
A ship! It's true!
Ha! ha! ha! This'll be the death of me!
Let's hope . . . let's hope they spot us!
!
SPLOSH
Who wasn't going to drink any sea-water? That'll teach him!
So you decided to have some after all!
Me? Not on your life! . . . Not a drop! . . . Glub!
Oh! The ship! She no see us! . . . She go! . . .
!
?

Thundering typhoons! He's right! . . . She's getting further away. Who's the bath-tub admiral commanding that crew of landlubbers?
What now? How can we attract their attention?
I've an idea! Has anyone got a mirror?
A mirror? What on earth for?
Here . . . I have one.
You like comb too?
Well done, Tintin! I never thought of it!
No thanks, only the mirror.
Blistering barnacles, go on! . . . Flash the sunlight straight in their eyes; they'll see us in the end.
Let's hope so! It's our last chance!
Flashing light to starboard, sir.
There, sir . . . Do you see it?
Yes, I see . . . A raft . . . with three men.
Hello? . . . Yes, Captain, go ahead . . . What? A raft with three shipwrecked sailors? By Lucifer . . . I . . . Wait, I'll come and see . . . Till then, not a word to my guests. I'm coming.
There, my lord . . . Do you see the signals they're making. Three of them, and a little dog.
By Lucifer! . . . Tintin and the bearded sailor . . . And a third ruffian! . . . But what about the message Mull Pasha just sent me?
Shall I alter course, sir?
A waste of time . . . They're just some more of those practical jokers who drift across the ocean in a nut-shell . . . You know, it's the three all the newspapers wrote about . . . They don't need anything. Proceed on your course.
But my lord Marquis . . .
I said proceed . . . Fire and brimstone! Where should we be if we stopped for all the rag-tag-and-bobtail who put out to sea for fun! . . . Proceed . . . And not a word of this to the passengers . . . You understand?

Marquis! . . . Yoohoo, Marquis!
Marquis, where are you?
Here! What is it?
Castaways, my dear fellow! Out there on a raft.
It's true, Marquis. Real castaways! How madly gay!
Yes, yes, I know . . . I . . . I've just given orders for the Captain to pick them up.
Oh, how gorgeous! I've always dreamed of seeing real castaways!
They're going about!
Saved!
They've seen us at last!
Saved! . . . Oh, what a beautiful morning!
That does it. Now this really is the Raft of the Medusa!
By Lucifer! What's to be done? They mustn't see me!
Hello? Yes, my lord Marquis . . . Your name's not to be mentioned in front of the castaways . . . Yes, m'lord.
In addition, I want you to remove these men at once - my guests are too inquisitive, and must have no contact with them.
Thundering typhoons! What a beautiful ship. A multi-millionaire's yacht!
And those fools think their troubles are over! Ha! ha! ha! That's a good joke!

Thundering typhoons! What a magnificent yacht! Whose is she? . . . Hey, are they having a carnival on board?
SHEHERAZADE
Almost . . . A fancy-dress ball . . . And what a bunch they are: high society, I can tell you; nothing but dukes, duchesses and film stars - all the nobs.
Per la Madonna! Can you believe it! . . . It's Tintin, and his friend the deep-sea fisherman, Paddock.
I must go and welcome them. Art must embrace the children of Adventure!
In the name of the Marquis di Gorgonzola welcome aboard, carissime mie!
Signora Castafiore! . . . Run for it! What shall we do? . . . Hop back on the raft?
My dear Tintin!
Delighted to see you again, my dear Padlock . . . er . . . Harrock.
. . . 'n roll, Signora Castoroili, Harrock'n-roll!
I'm so sorry, Signora, but his lordship has given orders: these poor men are completely exhausted. And then . . . there's the risk of infection, you know.
But my good man, I'm not ill!
A little later . . .
Well, Parker, have you questioned them?
Yes, m'lord. They were aboard a sambuk, being taken to Mecca . . .
. . . This morning, their boat was machine-gunned and set on fire by aircraft from Khemed. After shooting down one of the planes, they made themselves a raft. They then rescued the pilot of the aircraft.
Well done, Parker. Thank you.
If your lordship will pardon me, I think I should mention that Signora Castafiore, who knows the two castaways, welcomed them in your lordship's name.
Diavolo!
The Marquis di Gorgonzola's yacht! . . . It's fantastic . . . I must be dreaming.
Come on, Tintin . . . Up in the clouds again? . . . Hey! Tintin!

They can't stay here on board. But what's to be done? What indeed? . . . Ah, I have it! The "Ramona". . . . She's in these waters . . . Tomorrow we must pass one another, as if by chance.
Next day at dawn . . .
Get dressed quickly. You're in luck. We've met a merchantman bound for Mecca: just where you were making for. Her master has agreed to take you aboard.
Er . . . I . . . What . . . Good that's fine.
And a few minutes later . . .
RAMONA
PANAMA RP
So that's that! And now, my fine friends, I wish you a pleasant journey. Ha! ha! ha! ha!
Ah, this is the place for me: back aboard a good old freighter.
There, you two: these are your quarters. Your pal's going elsewhere . . . The skipper will be down to see you soon: he'll bring you your whisky himself!
Hi, you lubberly scum, not so fast! What do you mean?
This is too much! He's locked us in, the insolent porcupine!
Open up! Thundering typhoons, open up! You ill-mannered savages!
THUMP
THUMP
Well, well, you old drunkard! So you're kicking up a row already?
Allan!!
!

This is a happy reunion, eh, old bottle-nose? We must have a drink on it.
Allan! What's going on? How have we . . .
. . . ended up here? Quite simple: I command one of di Gorgonzola's freighters. Yesterday I had a signal ordering me to alter course. So this morning we met the "Scheherazade", as if by accident . . . Neatly done, eh?
Very! And may we inquire what you plan to do with us?
If you're sensible, you'll be put ashore. But not at Mecca . . . At Wadesdah!
Wadesdah! But that's murder! Sheik Bab El Ehr has put a price on our heads . . .
You're breaking my heart, dear boy. But that's enough talk . . . You must be thirsty . . . Here, drink my health . . .
Not on your life! . . . And you'll put us ashore at Mecca, or else!
Or else what? . . . Ha! ha! ha! . . . I advise you to behave yourselves. Don't forget we're in the Red Sea, and there's no shortage of sharks . . . You get me? . . . Now, like a big-hearted chap, I'll leave this bottle to console you.
'Bye for now! . . . We dock the day after tomorrow. So you've plenty of time to solve one important question: do you sleep with your beard under or over the sheet?
Ha! ha! ha! . . . That's a good one! His beard!
Yes, he won't sleep a wink tonight!
Over? . . . No, not that way . . .
Under? . . . Blistering barnacles! Not that way either!
!
Stay! . . . Once a drunkard . . .
. . . always a drunkard!
Go on! Just a little sip . . .
Well, why not?
CRASH

Over? . . .
Under? . . .
To Beelzebub with the bedclothes! I'm too hot anyway!
There . . . That's the answer!
Now for some sleep . . . at last.
BANG
THUMP
THIS WAY! HURRY! BANG
CLOMP
INTO THE BOATS!
There, I'm dreaming already!
COME ON, JOE!
BANG
Hey, this is no dream! . . . Those shouts . . . that stampeding . . . The engines have stopped . . . that's real enough!
Show a leg, there!
?
Did . . . did you fall out of your bunk?
Where d'you think I came from? . . . Mars? . . . Blistering barnacles, get up! . . . I think that bunch of rats are abandoning ship!
Open up, thundering typhoons! . . . Open up before I get violent!
Captain, this sea-chest. Let's try to force the door.
BUMP
BUMP
BUMP
7
Quick, let's see what's happening.
YEOW!
7
C. OLSSON
Hurry, Captain, hurry!
Thundering typhoons! The ship's on fire!
Keep it up, boys! Row hard! She'll blow up any minute.

Wreckers! . . . Pirates! . . . Filibusters! . . . Picaroons! Leaving us in the lurch on a doomed ship! To Davy Jones with the lot of you!
Follow me . . . We'll probably find a raft up for'ard.
We obviously have a vocation for shipwrecks!
HEY! HELP! HELP!
EFFENDI! EFFENDI!
There's someone in the hold! . . . What the . . . ?!
Who are you, below there?
We good black men . . . Want come out . . . No can breathe . . . We afraid . . .
Negroes! A lot of them, too, I'd say . . . What shall we do, Captain? We can't just abandon them.
You're right. Come on.
We'll try and put out the blaze . . . That cargo . . . I just can't make it out!
Eighteen tons of high explosive and ammunition: it'll make a pretty fireworks display!
That's it! The hose is connected . . . Now then, let's open the valve.
!
Blub . . . I . . . blub . . . I've got it, Cap . . . blub . . .
Thanks . . . that's it . . . I'll tackle the fire . . . You go over to port and get another hose into action.

Let's hope this will do the job!
What about the explosion? Is it due for today or . . . But . . . but . . . I can't see any more smoke or flames!
By thunder! The fire's gone out! Put her about boys. We're going back.
It . . . it's out . . . A huge wave . . . I was very nearly washed overboard . . .
What luck! . . . Now for those poor fellows below, Captain.
You're right, but first of all . . .
. . . I'm going to try to restart the engines. You go up on the bridge and take the wheel.
Half an hour later . . .
By thunder! . . . The "Ramona" is drawing away! . . . Someone has got her engines going!
Phew! that was no joke, alone; but she's under way at last.
Magnificent, Captain . . . And now for the Negroes.
There's something more urgent: to send out a distress call by radio.
!
OH!

Look!
Skut! . . . Dead?
No, he's alive . . . See, he's coming round.
Skut! Skut, old man, say something! What happened?
You escape! Hurry! . . . Hurry! . . . The fire! . . . Ship full of ammunition! . . . Hurry before explosion . . .
Ammunition! The pirates! . . . That's why they deserted like rats . . .
Don't worry, Skut: the fire's out. There's no more danger . . . But what about you? What happened?
They wake me, to go with them . . . Without you . . . I refuse . . . I want to . . . er . . . wake you . . . and send radio signal.
Then they are angry . . . Break radio and fight with me . . . Then I . . . knocked-out. They go?
Yes, they abandoned us, the iconoclasts. So here we are alone on board, with a crowd of Negroes in the hold.
You like . . . I can help you . . . Repair radio, perhaps, send S.O.S. . . .
Good idea . . . Do that . . . I'm going to make sure there's no further danger.
A little later . . .
No more need to worry, youngster: the fire is right out.
Now I'll take care of those Negroes. First, to let them out . . .
Save poor Muslim!
Me ill. Me dying.
All right! I'm coming now!
Hey there! . . . Let go of me!! . . . HELP, TINTIN! . . . HELP!
?
Troglodytes! . . . Sea-gherkins! . . . Pickled herrings! Leave me alone!
Back, visigoths! . . . Back, anacoluthons!
!
Hang on, Captain! . . . I'm coming! . . .

All right! I'm here!
So sorry, Captain, but I had no choice.
Please don't worry: I'm getting used to it!
You addle-pated lumps of anthracite, you! I let you out of that dungeon, and what thanks do I get? You knock me flat!
Effendi not be angry . . . You not shout . . . We not know you good white man . . . We think you bad white man who shut poor black man in bottom of ship . . . Where are bad white men?
Bad white men all gone. Left us. But if you help me, I'll take you wherever you want to go. You're going to Mecca, eh?
Yes, Effendi, to Mecca. We good Muslims. We making pilgrimage to the tomb of the Prophet.
All right, we'll take you to Mecca . . . on condition that you all obey my orders. For a start, I need some men as stokers.
Me, Effendi . . .
Me . . .
Me . . .
Me, Effendi . . .
Two days later . . .
There. If my reckoning is correct we should soon sight Jidda, the port for Mecca.
Yes. Those poor fellows . . . nearly the end of their journey.
Poor fellows! . . . Poor fellows! . . . You don't still believe they were being sold as slaves? . . . It's absurd . . .
If the Emir was telling the truth, then I'm afraid that was to be their fate.
Come, come, you've been reading too many thrillers . . . There's no slave-trading nowadays!
Look, Captain; just tell me this: is there any coke aboard?
Any . . . any coke? . . . But . . .
Effendi! Effendi! You come look! . . . Ship coming to us . . .
!

So it is! A sambuk . . . The harbour pilot from Jidda, perhaps . . . No, we're still too far from shore . . . A fisherman, then?
How odd . . . he's signalling to us . . . We'll heave to, and see what he wants . . .
Salaams, O sailor . . . Captain Allan is up there?
Captain Allan? . . . Finished . . . Gone . . . I am captain now.
Ah, you have replaced him . . . Good, good . . . Is the coke of best quality this time?
The coke?? Again? Blistering barnacles, what's all this nonsense about coke? Thundering typhoons, there's no coke on board!
No coke on board! . . . Ha! ha! ha!
Come here, you.
Yes, Effendi.
Hmm . . . Yes . . . Strong muscles . . . You'll do . . .
And teeth? . . . Come on, open your mouth, Sambo . . . Hmm, not too bad . . . Teeth quite sound . . .
?
!
Here, have you quite finished playing the cattle-dealer? This man's not a horse, nor a slave . . .
Ssh! . . . You mustn't say that! . . . "Coke" is the word, as you well know.
Coke!! . . . Blistering barnacles! . . . Tintin was right! There still are slave-traders . . . And that's what you're up to, you brute!
You trafficker in human flesh! You deserve to be strung up on the mizzen yardarm!

LOOK OUT!
!
?
ZZINNG
You cut-throat, you! . . . You're lucky I don't stuff your beard down your gullet! . . . But get out . . . viper! And take care that you don't cross my path again!
Sheer off, filibuster! . . . Out of my sight, you gallows bird!
Baboon! . . . Carpet-seller! . . . Paranoiac! . . . Pockmark! . . . Cannibal!
RAMONA
Duck-billed platypus! . . . Jellied-eel! . . . Bashi-bazouk! . . . Anthropophagus! . . . Cercopithecus! . . . Psychopath! . . . Er . . .
No good, Captain. He's too far away now . . .
That's what you think! He hasn't heard the last of me!
Where now?
On to the bridge.
PIRATE!
ECTOPLASM
COELACANTH
VULTURE!
BODY-SNATCHER!
OSTROGOTH!
VANDAL!
This time I think he really is out of earshot.
Yes! . . . More's the pity . . . dirty slave-trader!
By the way . . . How did you tumble to the word "coke"?
I'll show you.
I found this scrap of paper on the table while you were plotting our course on the chart. Read it.
di Gorgonzola to Captain A
Ramona
Deliver Coke to the
el Kaid at Jidda
By the beard of the Prophet, the dog will pay dearly for this!

A fragment of a wireless message sent by di Gorgonzola to that gangster Allan! . . . And "coke" is a code word for their cargo of slaves! . . . The pirates!
First, we must talk to the Africans: they must be made to understand that under the circumstances it's madness for them to go to Mecca.
Agreed . . . Then we must try to send out a radio call . . .
Getting on, Skut?
Still much work, Captain.
Good . . . Well, I'm going to talk to the cargo. You take the wheel and steer due south. We'll head for Djibouti.
OK
A few minutes later . . .
My friends, listen to me carefully. You have undertaken this long journey to make a pilgrimage to Mecca, haven't you?
Yes.
Yes.
Afterwards, of course, you plan to return home and rejoin your families. Isn't that so?
Yes, Effendi.
Yes.
Yes.
I'm afraid a very different fate awaits you. You saw that Arab who came aboard, and I chased off? . . . He's waiting for you in Mecca, to buy you and make you into slaves! . . . Slaves, you understand?
You speak well, Effendi. Wicked Arab, very wicked. Poor black men not want to be slaves. Poor black men want to go to Mecca.
Naturally, I realise that. But I repeat, if you go there, you'll be sold as slaves. Is that what you want?
We not slaves, Effendi. We good Muslims. We want to go to Mecca.
But billions of blue blistering barnacles, I keep on telling you: if you go there, you'll be sold as slaves! Thundering typhoons, I can't make it any clearer.
You not shout, Effendi. Poor black men only want to go to Mecca.
All right, you boneheads, go to Mecca! . . . But you'll stay there for ever! . . . You'll never see your own country again! . . . Never see your families again! . . . You'll be slaves for ever! . . . That's what you're in for, you dunderheaded coconuts, you!
We not coconuts, Effendi. We good black men. We good Muslims. We want to go to Mecca.
I can't do a thing! . . . I've tried the lot! . . . You can't shift them: they want to go to Mecca, stop: that's all! . . . It's like banging your head against a brick wall!

Emyny sofoyi ooiboo-yi konychééré!
Yirō!
Beyni!
Loyotō!
?
Now then . . . What's going on? . . . Why all the quarrelling?
I not want to go to Mecca. I tell them you are good white man, you speak truth. I remember in my village three young men went to Mecca . . . Two years ago . . . They not come back . . . They no doubt slaves . . . I not want to go to Mecca! . . . I not want to be slave.
Me too, I not go.
Me too!
Good, so I haven't preached in vain! . . . All right, we'll make a bargain: those who don't want to go to Mecca will be landed at another port. As for the rest, they can continue the voyage if they want to . . .
Good, Effendi.
The next morning . . .
There . . . the day after tomorrow we'll be at Djibouti, and that'll be the end of our worries . . .
Yes, if all goes well! I shan't be really happy till we get there. You can bet that at this very moment di Gorgonzola is aware of the situation. And he knows that we know . . . Watch out for what he's cooking up! . . .
BRRRRR
?
!
An aeroplane . . . They're circling us . . . how odd . . .
Hello, hello . . . Albatross to Shark . . . Have sighted Ramona 20 miles west of the Farasan Islands . . . She is steering south-south-east. Over.
ADF
Hello, hello . . . Shark to Albatross . . . Message received . . . Steering west . . .
. . . to intercept her . . . Out.
Aha! My orders have been carried out.
He's going off . . . I wonder what he was up to.
I don't know, but I don't much care for that sort of visit.
The trap is closing: my boys are on the job! . . . In a few hours the "Ramona" will have disappeared, with crew and cargo . . . So all the incriminating evidence will be effectively liquidated.

That plane snooping around worries me . . . If I were you, Captain, I'd alter course.
You're right . . . I'll do so.
A few hours later . . .
Well, Skut, how's the radio? Working?
No . . .
No! . . . The radio not working . . . I not find the trouble . . . I not know what more to do . . .
BRRRRR
Again? . . .
The same one? . . .
Be careful, the wire!
OH!
?
The radio! Quite all broken now!
!
?
Hello . . . Albatross to Shark . . . Have found Ramona again.
Steering due south; she is 30 miles east of Dahlak-kebir Island.
That bird of ill-omen is getting on my nerves.
Buzz off, you stool-pigeon! You're asking for a smack on the nose!
!
Shark to Albatross. Ramona in sight. Preparing to dive.

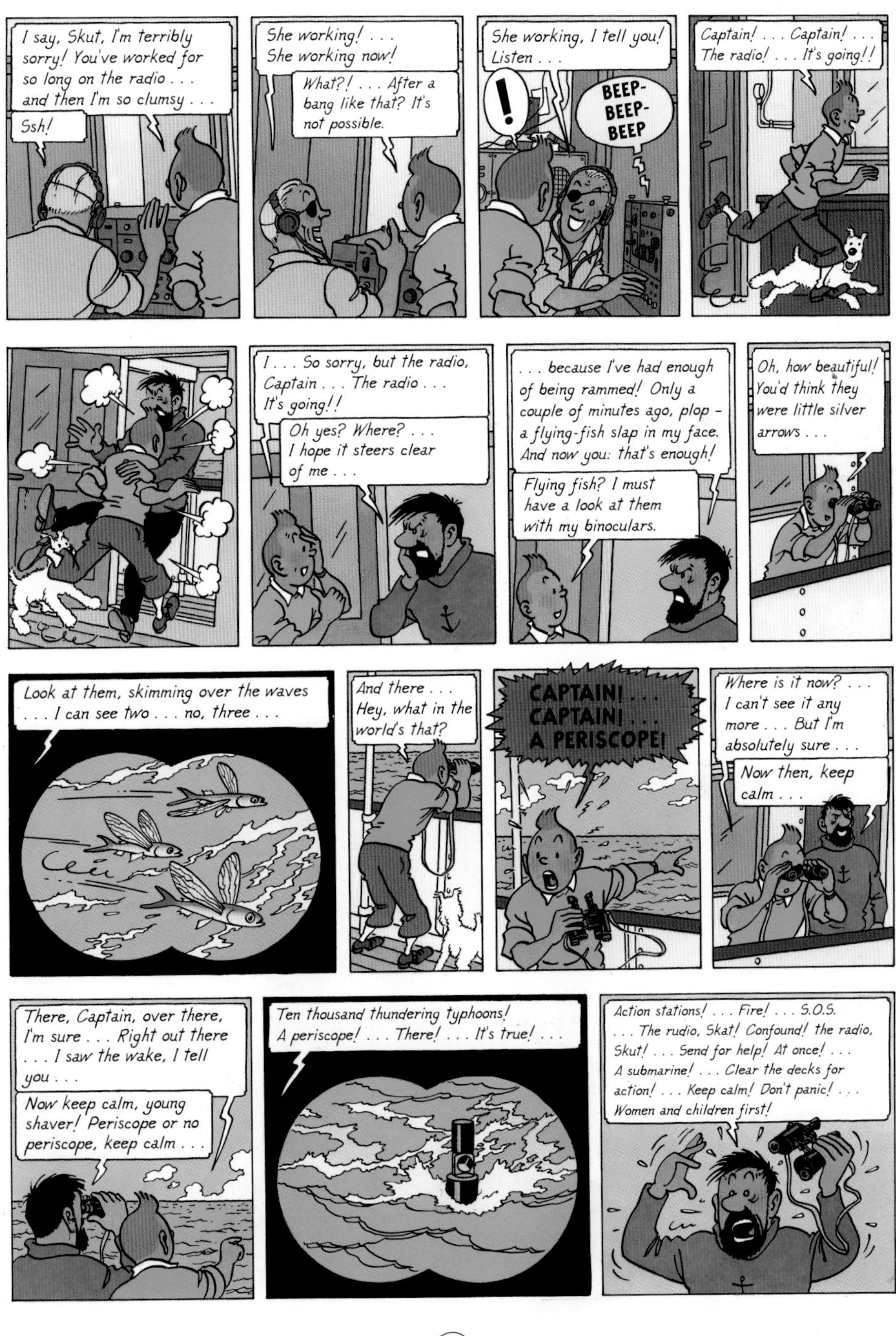
I say, Skut, I'm terribly sorry! You've worked for so long on the radio . . . and then I'm so clumsy . . .
Ssh!
She working! . . . She working now!
What?! . . . After a bang like that? It's not possible.
She working, I tell you! Listen . . .
!
BEEP-BEEP-BEEP
Captain! . . . Captain! . . . The radio! . . . It's going!!
I . . . So sorry, but the radio, Captain . . . The radio . . . It's going!!
Oh yes? Where? . . . I hope it steers clear of me . . .
. . . because I've had enough of being rammed! Only a couple of minutes ago, plop - a flying-fish slap in my face. And now you: that's enough!
Flying fish? I must have a look at them with my binoculars.
Oh, how beautiful! You'd think they were little silver arrows . . .
Look at them, skimming over the waves . . . I can see two . . . no, three . . .
And there . . . Hey, what in the world's that?
CAPTAIN! . . . CAPTAIN! . . . A PERISCOPE!
Where is it now? . . . I can't see it any more . . . But I'm absolutely sure . . .
Now then, keep calm . . .
There, Captain, over there, I'm sure . . . Right out there . . . I saw the wake, I tell you . . .
Now keep calm, young shaver! Periscope or no periscope, keep calm . . .
Ten thousand thundering typhoons! A periscope! . . . There! . . . It's true! . . .
Action stations! . . . Fire! . . . S.O.S. . . . The rudio, Skat! Confound! the radio, Skut! . . . Send for help! At once! . . . A submarine! . . . Clear the decks for action! . . . Keep calm! Don't panic! . . . Women and children first!

Calm down, Captain, calm down! ... All isn't lost yet!
You're right ... Keep cool ... keep calm and don't panic!
Disaster! ... The end! ... There's nothing we can do! If they're di Gorgonzola's people we're finished!
But why?
The ammunition! ... In the forward hold ... A torpedo in there, and you know the rest!
Of course! Only the torpedo isn't here yet! Come on, hurry; everyone on the alert.
Not far away ...
We're almost within range ... They don't know what's in store for them.
This won't take long to settle ... Stand by No. 1 tube ...
Tintin at the radio. You at the wheel, Skut. Repeat my orders when I give them. Remember, starboard is right; port on the left ...
S.O.S. ... S.O.S. ... s.s. Ramona calling. Unidentified submarine in immediate vicinity. ... We fear the worst ... Here is our position.
No. 1 tube, fire!
S.O.S. ... S.O.S. ... s.s. Ramona calling ... In danger of being torpedoed ...
Torpedo to port! Hard a starboard! ...
Hard a starboard it is!
Curses on them! They've swung away ... They must have spotted us.
S.O.S. ... S.O.S. ... A torpedo has just missed us ... S.O.S. ... Hurry please ... S.O.S.
A moment later, aboard the U. S. S. Los Angeles ...
An S.O.S. I just picked up, sir.
What's all this ballyhoo about a submarine? ... There isn't a war on, is there?
But meanwhile ...
Starboard 20 ... Ahead, speed six knots ... Stand by No. 2 tube.

Hooray! Someone's heard our call!
U.S.S. Los Angeles to s.s. Ramona. Your S.O.S. received. We are coming to your assistance. Will be with you in three hours.
We've managed to miss the first torpedo, but we'll probably be done for before you get here.
There they are ahead, to port. This time they won't escape us . . .
By rights he should be astern, to starboard. In a few minutes I'll turn to port again, to confuse him.
Peer sport 30° . . . I mean steer port 30°.
Port 30° it is.
By the powers of Satan! They've dodged us again!
Wait now! He'll end up by turning to starboard again . . . And then . . .
Submarine obviously belongs to the slave-traders. Their leader is the Marquis di Gorgonzola, now aboard m.s. Scheherazade, cruising in the Red Sea.
Starboard 45°.
Starboard 45° it is.
Right! . . . No. 2 tube, fire!
Torpedo to starboard! Thundering typhoons! Quick, the engine-room telegraph . . .
Blistering barnacles! Full speed ahead!
STOP
SLOW
HALF
FULL
!
Billions of blue blistering barnacles!

Thundering typhoons! The engine-room telegraph is jammed at half-speed astern. Quick, a screw-driver!
By Lucifer! They're going astern . . . our torpedo has missed again . . . They're tough, those boys . . .
Hooray! It's passed ahead of us.
S.O.S. A second torpedo has just missed. Hurry, Los Angeles.
Quick! Quick! I must release this infernal machine!
PCHKRAAPRVT! . . . TRRKHKRAA! . . . You confounded rattletrap . . .
. . . tin-can contraption! . . . Take that!
YEEOWW!
Ah, they're still going astern! Very well! No. 3 and No. 4 tubes ready?
CLING
CLANG
Take that, you slot-machine, you!
?
Hello? . . . Engine room? . . . Hello?
Hello, Effendi?
BRROM
Too late! . . . They've got us!

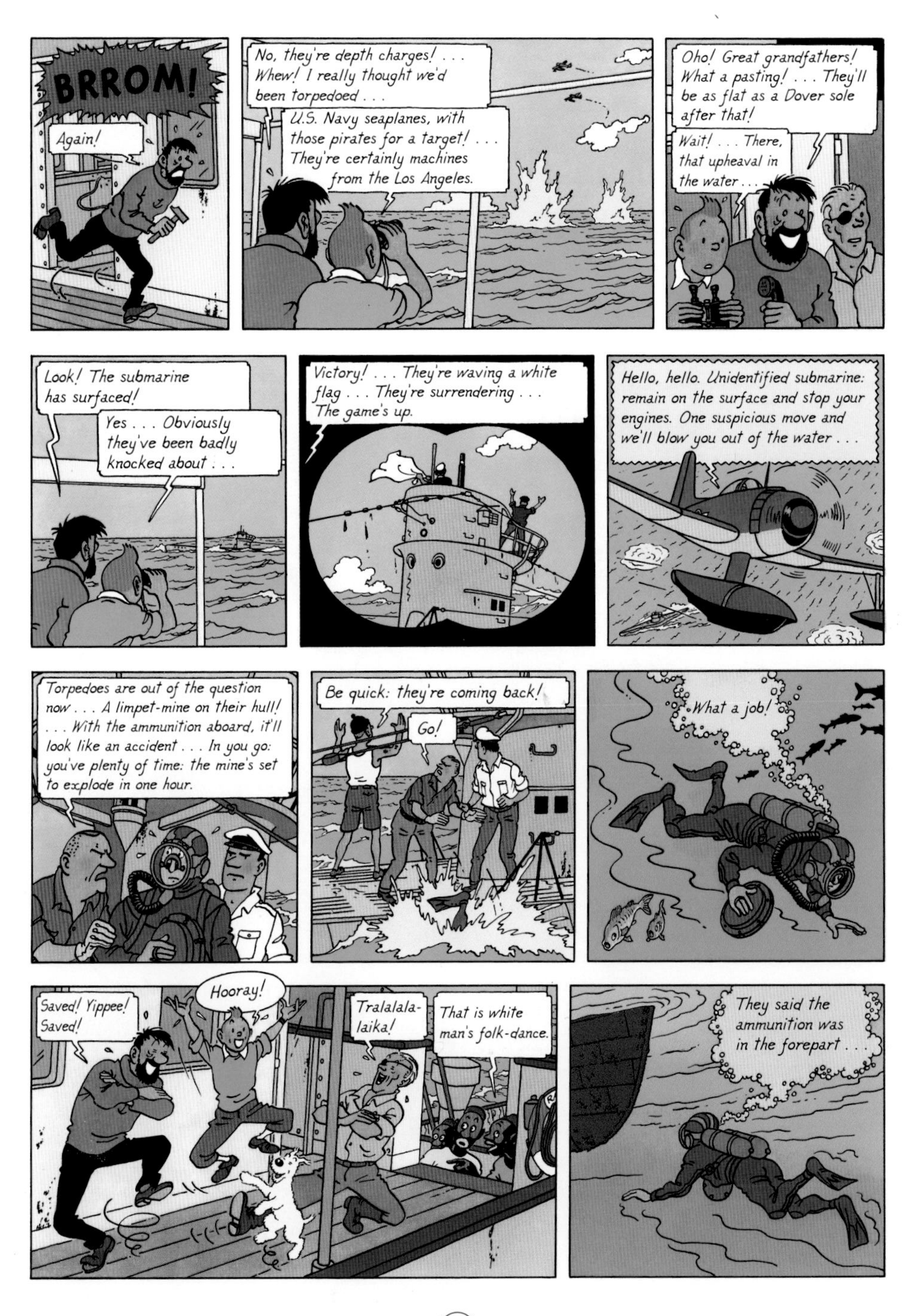
BRROM!
Again!
No, they're depth charges! . . . Whew! I really thought we'd been torpedoed . . .
U.S. Navy seaplanes, with those pirates for a target! . . . They're certainly machines from the Los Angeles.
Oho! Great grandfathers! What a pasting! . . . They'll be as flat as a Dover sole after that!
Wait! . . . There, that upheaval in the water . . .
Look! The submarine has surfaced!
Yes . . . Obviously they've been badly knocked about . . .
Victory! . . . They're waving a white flag . . . They're surrendering . . . The game's up.
Hello, hello. Unidentified submarine: remain on the surface and stop your engines. One suspicious move and we'll blow you out of the water . . .
Torpedoes are out of the question now . . . A limpet-mine on their hull! . . . With the ammunition aboard, it'll look like an accident . . . In you go: you've plenty of time: the mine's set to explode in one hour.
Be quick: they're coming back!
Go!
What a job!
Saved! Yippee! Saved!
Hooray!
Tralalalalaika!
That is white man's folk-dance.
They said the ammunition was in the forepart . . .

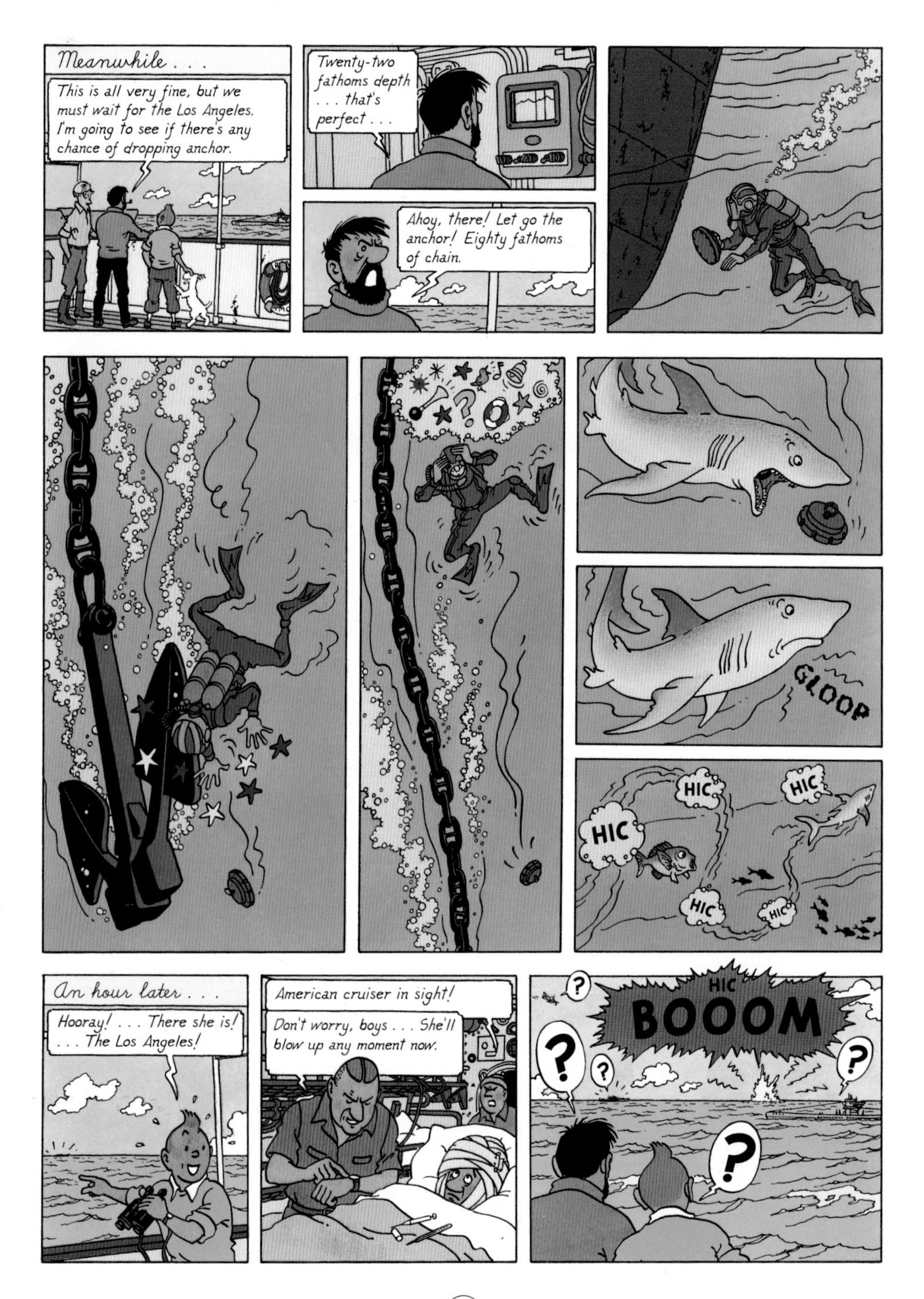
Meanwhile . . .
This is all very fine, but we must wait for the Los Angeles. I'm going to see if there's any chance of dropping anchor.
Twenty-two fathoms depth . . . that's perfect . . .
Ahoy, there! Let go the anchor! Eighty fathoms of chain.
GLOOP
HIC
HIC
HIC
HIC
HIC
An hour later . . .
Hooray! . . . There she is! . . . The Los Angeles!
American cruiser in sight!
Don't worry, boys . . . She'll blow up any moment now.
HIC
BOOOM
?
?
?
?
?

The next morning . . .
Still no news from Kurt and his submarine . . . What are they playing at, the fools?
. . . and naval craft to intercept the m.s. Scheherazade and arrest the owner, name of Rastapopoulos, alias the Marquis di Gorgonzola . . .
Lost . . . all is lost! . . . But it's impossible!
RRING
RRING
Hello? . . . Yes . . . Come up on the bridge? . . . I haven't time, Captain. I . . . What? . . . A warship? . . . I . . . I'm coming now.
The cruiser Los Angeles, my lord Marquis . . . She's just flashed a signal ordering us to heave to. What shall I do?
Repeat the message, Tom . . . And add that if they don't heave to immediately, we'll open fire.
All right. Stop the engines. And launch my personal barge. I'll go myself and tell those insolent cowboys what I think of their manners! . . .
Ah, they've obeyed . . . Excellent! . . . But what are they doing now? . . .
It looks as if . . . yes, they're hoisting out a launch . . . and Rastapopoulos is going aboard . . .
Do not insist, my friends. I will go alone.
SHEHERAZADE
. . . And he's steering towards us! . . . Well, this beats everything! . . . To have the cheek to come and brazen it out! What a nerve!
But what's happening now? . . . He's slowing up. He's stopping . . . Has he broken down?
Great snakes! . . . He's sinking! . .
Whoops! That's done the trick! . . . Just you catch me now gentlemen! . . . Ha! ha! ha!

NEW REVELATIONS SHOCK WORLD
SLAVERY—IT STILL EXISTS
Traffickers in human lives use code-word "COKE"
EMIR BEN KALISH EZAB
MULL PASHA
Revolutionary Leader
Mull Pasha
CAPTAIN ALLAN
Picked up by Danish Cargo Vessel
Where did Sheik Bab El Ehr get his Warplanes?
WAR SURPLUS STOCKS ACQUIRED BY DAWSON ON BEHALF OF RASTAPOPOULOS
UNITED NATIONS APPEAL
Delegates demand international control of Mecca pilgrimage transport
PIRATE SUBMARINE IN RED SEA
TINTIN IN NEW
A fortnight later . . .
Well, what a joy to be home again, and to breathe the country air . . .
. . . and hear the old familiar sounds . . . Listen: the sound of a motor; it's the gardener mowing the lawn . . .
POF
ZZZZZZZZZ
POF

?
ZZING
BANG
BONG
Great snakes! It's Professor Calculus! . . . What's he invented this time?!
Hello there, Professor! That's certainly a funny way to welcome people!
So there you are! Welcome back to Marlinspike.
What on earth are those contraptions?
Ingenious, aren't they?
Motor-roller-skates. For a long time I've been trying to find an answer to the traffic problem . . . I was thinking of a flexible, handy, lightweight machine . . .
?
Fine! . . . And they'll have to install traffic lights on the pavements with your confounded roller-coasters! . . . But where is Abdullah?
No, a two-stroke engine, of 48 c.c.s, and controlled by cables which regulate the throttle and steer the skates at the same time.
That's all very interesting . . . But I asked you, where is Abdullah? . . . Abdullah? WHERE IS ABDULLAH?
You simply won't believe it, but I've reached 40 m.p.h.! . . . Would you like to try them?
Oh, sir!! . . . Oh, how glad I am to see you back, sir!!
Hello, Nestor, I . . . But my poor Nestor, what's happened to you?
I . . . I fear that Master Abdullah's visit was not very good for me . . . But things are better now . . . He and his retinue departed yesterday. He left a note for you.
Poor Nestor! . . . A real demon, that boy. Let's see what he's written to us.
Can't he use my proper name?
To dear Blistring Barniculs.
"My dear Blistering Barnacles, I have been very good. I haven't played any jokes. Papa wrote to me. I must go home. That's sad, because it is fun at Marlinspike. With love from Abdullah."
Very sweet, eh? . . . Nestor's just been fussing about a little innocent childish mischief.
BANG

Billions of bilious blue blistering barnacles in a thundering typhoon! Another joke by that infernal child . . . Shall I never be left in peace?! In peace!!
Sir, Mr Wagg has just arrived . . .
Who? . . . Jolyon Wagg? . . . Oh, no, no! . . . I want some peace! . . . Peace!
Hello, old boy! How are you, you old sea-dog? I'm doing fine . . . in the pink! . . . Ha! ha! ha! ha! . . . What a lark to see you again, you old humbug, you!
Er . . .
Well, my old salt, I've got a surprise for you . . . I know the country's pretty, but it's dull as ditchwater . . .
A matter of taste . . .
No, no, take it from me, it's dull. So I said to myself: "Jolyon," I said, "you must go and liven things up for that old stick-in-the-mud . . ."
That's very kind of you, but . . .
Now, now, turn it up! No buts! Too easy. I'm president of the Vagabond Car Club down my way; all I've had to do is organise a rally, and the final trials . . .
. . . are at Marlinspike!
START
CONTROL
THE END

HERGÉ

★

THE ADVENTURES OF

TINTIN

★

Tintin in Tibet

LITTLE, BROWN AND COMPANY
New York Boston

Tintin in Tibet

What a glorious holiday, eh, Snowy?

Call this a holiday! . . . Scrambling over jagged rocks from morning till night. All right for him, with his heavy climbing boots. But if this goes on I'll have no paws left!

It's been a long day: I'm not sorry to be back at the hotel. I'm hungry as a hunter.
HOTEL DES SOMMETS

Hello, Captain. Had a good day?
Marvellous, thanks. What about you? Fagged out, I'll bet!

A bit tired, I must say, but on top of the world. The mountains are superb . . . and the air's like champagne. You ought to come with me one day . . .

Who, me??

Not on your life! I don't mind mountains as scenery; but this passion for clambering about over piles of rock, that's what beats me! Besides, you've always got to come down again. What's it all in aid of, anyway?
A broken neck, I suppose? But no one ever thinks of the risk. You're always seeing accidents in the papers: mountain drama here, Alpine disaster there. Mountains should be abolished. At least that'd stop all these aeroplanes bumping into every other peak . . .

It's just happened again . . . in Nepal. I was reading the story in the paper. Here . . . look.

NEPAL AIR DISASTER

KATMANDU, Wednesday.—The D.C.3 missing since Monday on a flight from Patna to Katmandu is reported to have crashed in the Gosain Than massif.

It is believed that the aircraft, belonging to Indian Airways, was driven towards the Himalaya by a violent storm.

A search-plane yesterday spotted the wreckage of the aircraft in a remote and dangerous area. As soon as the news was received, a party of Sherpas set out for the peak where the aircraft crashed.

The aircraft is known to have carried 14 passengers and 4 crew.

BANDITS IN VIENNA RAID

Billions of blue blistering barnacles! You don't really have to sneeze like that, do you?
But . . . I . . . I . . . didn't sneeze.
I'm terribly sorry. I must have dropped off . . . I had a horrible nightmare . . .
A nightmare?
Yes. I was dreaming about Chang . . . you remember Chang, the boy I made friends with in China . . . I saw him . . . it was ghastly . . .
He was lying there hurt, half buried by snow . . . He was holding out his hands and calling to me, "Help, Tintin! help!" It was all so terribly real . . . I'm still quite stunned by it . . . Please do forgive me.
That's all right, don't worry. Forget it. You go on up to bed. You're dead tired.
I think you're right. Good night, Captain.
The next morning . . .
Hello there! Slept well?. . . No more dreams?
Good morning, Captain. No, no more dreams.
No dreams, but not much sleep, either. I was haunted by that picture of Chang lying in the snow, calling to me for help.
Rubbish! Dreams go by opposites, so they say. Don't think about it. Look, there's a letter for you, from Hong Kong.
Hong Kong?
Yes, look at the envelope. It's taken a long time to reach you. From Labrador Road to Marlinspike, then Nestor sent it on here.
Who's writing to me from Hong Kong?
BY AIR MAIL
PAR AVION
丁丁先生台啟
比國布魯塞尔
香港張仲文
Please forward:
Mr. Tintin
Hotel des Sommets,
Vargèse
CHANG!
!

Honestly! Billions of blue blistering barnacles! You can't pretend this time that you've had another dream!
No, no! Look here: it really is a letter from Chang!
You must admit it's a remarkable coincidence. Yesterday evening I dreamt about him: this morning I get a letter from him. Extraordinary, isn't it?
Yes . . . I suppose so. What does he want, anyway?
Here, listen: "The brother of my most venerable adoptive father" . . . I didn't know that Mr Wang Chen-Yee had a brother . . . "The brother of my most venerable adoptive father is living in London, where he has an antique shop. He has generously invited me to stay with him . . ." Hooray!
"Although unworthy of such an invitation I have accepted. Tomorrow I leave Hong Kong by air. I am filled with pleasure that I shall see your noble face once again." He's coming! Good!
Yes, fine . . . But, I say . . . this Chang, he's not like that little monster Abdullah, is he?
Chang? Why, Captain, he's one of the nicest people I know: quiet, unassuming - and with a heart of gold. You'll see!
Yes, and Chang's an old friend of yours too, isn't he, Snowy?
Professor Calculus! Wonderful news! Chang's coming! We're going to see CHANG again!
Champagne? At this hour!?
Chang's coming! . . . Tralala!
It is most reprehensible, Captain, to give this young man champagne, and in the morning too!
?
When's he coming, then . . . your . . . er . . . Son of Heaven?
Let's see.
He says: "I fly to Calcutta, then on to Nepal. My venerable adoptive father wishes me to visit Katmandu to pay my respects to his honourable cousin who has many children, and to take them presents."
Nepal? . . . Katmandu? . . . The plane that hit a mountain . . . surely that was going to Katmandu?
Quick . . . this morning's paper. Perhaps there'll be some details of the crash.
Daily Reporter

There! "Nepal Air Disaster - No survivors."
on the passe... addition to 4 members of the crew.
TRAGIC DELAY
Among the missing is a young Chinese, travelling from Hong Kong to London. He arrived in Patna in time for an earlier aircraft but failed to obtain a seat. Forced to wait overnight, he caught the ill-fated D.C.3. The victim of this tragic delay is Chang Chong-Chen, adopted son of Mr. Wang Chen-... had arranged
Oil we... discov... and e... new
Chang! . . . My poor friend, Chang!
That's what comes of drinking too much champagne!
You . . . you and your champagne!
Chang! My dear friend Chang! We shall never see him again . . . never again!
No, it isn't true! . . . I know . . . CHANG IS NOT DEAD!
Not dead??
He's alive; I'm sure of it! . . . The accident happened days ago, but yesterday I saw Chang alive . . . calling for help, but alive!
But that was just a dream you had . . . it wasn't real.
I know. But it wasn't an ordinary dream. It was . . . it was a sort of premonition . . . telepathy . . . something like that. But one thing's certain; I know that Chang is alive.
Steady on, Tintin.
He's alive, I tell you! I'm packing my bag and leaving for Nepal.
What?. . . You?. . . Leaving for Nepal?
But look here, old fellow, it's madness! . . .
That's right! You go and sober up!
Tintin, listen. I can understand how grieved you are, and I realise how much that dream has shaken you, but you must be sensible . . .
I must save Chang!
Ten thousand thundering typhoons! How can you possibly save someone who's already dead?
Chang is not dead.
CHANG!
!
?

Chang, come here! How often must I tell you not to speak to common mongrels?
Blistering barnacles! What a daft idea, giving a name like that to a dog!
Not really: it's a Pekingese, it's quite reasonable.
Look here, Tintin . . . If your friend Chang was still alive, then the rescue party would have found him.
Possibly . . .
A common mongrel! Me!!
Possibly! . . . Possibly! . . . All right, let's suppose that he is still alive. I . . .
!
?
CHANG
Do you really have to sneeze like that?
Excuse be, sir, but I'b got a terrible cold id by dose . . .
CHANG
As I was saying: even if he were alive, why should you be able to find him, when Sherpas and experienced mountaineers have failed?
Captain, I am convinced that Chang is alive. Maybe it's stupid, but there it is. And since I believe that he's alive, I'm going to look for him.
All right, be obstinate! Go to Nepal, go to Timbuctoo, go to Vladivostok for all I care! But you'll be on your own, remember; I'm not coming and that's flat! And when I say no, I mean no!
Two days later, at New Delhi . . .
VT-DAO

A few minutes later . . .
The plane for Katmandu? . . . Oh yes, calling at Patna. It leaves at 2.35 this afternoon, but from the other airport, Willingdon. The bus will take you there, unless you . . .
. . . would rather visit the city. You have three hours. You should be at the airport at 2.00 p.m. You will find your baggage there.
Thank you. We'll take your advice and have a look round the city.
A little later . . .
There's the Qutab Minar. It's 238 feet high.
. . . and the Red Fort.
Three hours have passed . . .
We still haven't seen the Jama Masjid and the Rajghat, the memorial to Mahatma Gandhi . . .
Yes, but aren't you forgetting the time?
We've just got time to hop into a taxi and make a dash for the airport.
Pity!
Hello, there's a crowd down there. What's going on? A fight? Or an accident? . . .
A cow! She's certainly chosen a good spot . . . completely blocking the roadway.
I say, can't someone move the old girl along? We're in rather a hurry . . .
Sacred cow, Sahib . . . Do not disturb . . . You wait till she move.
Wait? That's a useful suggestion! Our plane leaves in twenty-five minutes.
Anyway, no need to worry: if she won't move we'll just step over her . . .
Hey! Whoa! Stop fooling around!
Hey! . . . Hi! . . . WHOA! . . . STOP!

PAINTS & CO
WOOAH!
HOOO! . . . STOP!
?
Where d'you think you're going?
I don't know! Ask the cow!
WOOAH! WOOAH!
Help! I've had enough! Put me down!
WOOAH! WOOAH!
?
TAXIS
Good afternoon . . . Where to, Sahib?
Where . . . er . . . Oh, yes. To the airport. But not right away: I'm waiting for a friend.
Here he comes at last!
Now, to Willingdon Airport . . . and step on it! We've got to be there in a quarter of an hour.
Trust me, Sahib . . .
. . . best taxi in Delhi, Sahib. Nothing can stop me!

Billions of blistering barnacles!
What's the matter?
Thundering typhoons! Something in my eye. I don't know what it is . . . dust, or a fly, or something. Stop, driver, stop!
No, I can't see anything. You'll have to wait until we're aboard the plane.
Carry on driver! And try to make up for lost time!
Right, Sahib.
THE BENGAL CO.
DELHI
Hey, my cap!
We go on like this, Sahib, and we never arrive in time.
CO
At the airport . . .
Can't be helped: it's time for take-off. Too bad for the two missing passengers.
AIR
No, look: here they come.
Blue blistering barnacles! Confound this thing in my eye!
AIR INDIA
AIR INDIA
That's lucky: I can just see enough to get up the gangway . . .
AIR INDIA
Captain, stop! Not there! Here! The other steps!
And when I've finished, I'll see what's in your eye.
FIRST AID

The next morning . . .
This is Katmandu.
First of all we'll see the airport manager.
There it is. We are friends of Chang, one of the victims of the Gosain Than disaster. We want to visit the scene of the crash. You know all about the organisation of the search party: can you help us to achieve our object? . . .
Would it be indiscreet to ask the reason why you wish to go up there?
Because I am certain that Chang is not dead. I want to go and look for him.
But you must be mad. You have no conception of the difficulty and the danger such an expedition involves.
That rubber band's getting on my nerves.
Not only would you be risking your lives, but the risk would be quite futile. Even if your friend survived the accident he would long since have died from hunger and cold and exposure.
That's what I keep on telling him.
Ha! ha! ha! ha!
Oh, sorry!
Look, sir . . . Chang is my friend. In spite of all appearances, I know that he is still alive. Whatever the obstacles lying in our path, I must try to find him.
Very well . . . I'm quite certain no guide will agree to go with you. But if you wish, I'll put you in touch with the Sherpas who made up the rescue party.
I really am very grateful.
You see? Anybody with any sense thinks as I do: this idea of yours is absolutely crazy!
Chang is alive, Captain!
Chang is alive! Chang is alive! All this just because you had a dream about him! . . . I dreamt about Columbus last night, but that doesn't bring him to life, does it? I don't behave like a sleep-walker, roaming around in a daze with my eyes shut!
Look out!
?

Wake up, you milk-maid, and look where you're going!
LOOK OUT!
Billions of blistering barnacles in a thundering typhoon! You did that on purpose, you gang of Bashi-bazouks!
क्यों जी? देखते नहीं सामने क्या है?...
What's the matter, Captain? Met your match at last?
Come on. We'll ask these men . . . perhaps they know the shop kept by Chang's relation.
Excuse me, but can you direct me to a shop owned by a Chinese gentleman . . . er . . . a Chinese shop?
Chinese shop?
I wonder what they are, those red mats over there.
Hello! It's fruit, spread out to dry in the sun. Mm! It smells good!
Fruit?. . . Good to eat?. . . Nice and sweet?. . . Yum-yum?
Yes, Sahib.
Yes, Sahib.
Chinese shop?. . . Up there, Sahib. You turn left. Then big temple . . . Then street right. There Chinese shop . . . Cheng Li is name.
Thank you very much.
FIRE!. . .

?
W-w-what happened? I ate one of those things. It was just like swallowing a volcano in full blast!
It was a red pimento, Captain . . . pepper! . . .
A few minutes later . . .
There's the big temple he mentioned . . .
Wonderful, isn't it?
Good-day Sahib. My name Cheng Li-Kin. I think you are looking for me . . . Yes please.
!
Yes . . . but how did you know?
Yes please, Sahib. You ask someone the way, and he come and tell me . . . Yes? . . .
Please to do me the inexpressible honour of taking a humble cup of tea in my miserable house. Yes please?
We'd be glad to. Yes please.
Mr Cheng, we are friends of Chang . . .
Friends of Chang? . . . So? . . . Yes please! . . . He will have great happiness to see you.
?
?

What . . . what did you say?
Great happiness to see you. Please to enter: we are here . . .
CHANG! CHANG! Some friends for you.
My son, Chang Lin-Yee . . . Yes please.
We're so sorry: there has been a mistake. Our friend is called Chang Chon-Chen.
Ah, you speak of our late lamented adoptive nephew . . . Yes please.
Alas! He is dead . . . Yes please . . . in aeroplane crash.
So we have heard. But I believe that Chang is not dead. I have come to ask . . . Do you know of a Sherpa who'd agree to go with us to search for Chang?
Even though he is dead?
I do not believe that. But I need an experienced guide if I am to find him.
Why not Tharkey, respected father? He is the best Sherpa in the district, and the bravest. Also, he went with the rescue party.
We go to him, if you wish. But I tell you his answer.
NO, SAHIB!
No! Me not want to risk three lives - your life, life of the other Sahib, and my life - to look for dead man.
But you see, Tharkey, I am convinced that Chang isn't dead.
Him dead, Sahib! . . . I go there. I see broken aeroplane. No one alive. Not possible to live: too cold, nothing to eat. You not go, Sahib, you too young to die as well.
It's only common sense, old lad. The Sherpa is absolutely right. I've told you from the very beginning, it's sheer lunacy. You really must give up this daft idea.
Yes, what Tharkey says is true.
Fine! You're talking sense at last!

It's true: I have no right to risk the lives of others.
Bravo! I knew you'd see reason.
I shall go alone.
!?
All right! . . . Go! . . . But on your own! I've trailed along this far, thundering typhoons, but I'm not playing nurse- maid any longer!
Look out, Captain!
Billions of bilious blue blistering barnacles! Has the word gone around to gang up on me? . . .
?!?
क्या? फिर वही?
Please, please . . . Watch your language! I didn't shout at you, did I?
Three days later . . .
There. That's my rucksack packed. Now I'll just say goodbye to the Captain.
I don't like the look of all these preparations.
RAT TAT TAT
YES?
!
?
I . . . I've come to say goodbye. But . . . your rucksack . . . What . . . ?
D'you imagine for one moment that I'd let a young whippersnapper like you go off alone? Not on your life! I suppose you think that Captain Haddock has got tomato juice in his veins, eh?
But you . . .
But, but, but . . . don't start being awkward! I'm going with you, whether you like it or not. And not another word from you, or I stay here!
Now who is it? Come in!
RAT TAT TAT
!?

Hey, you're the rogue who knocks me down at every street corner. Blistering barnacles, what do you want now?!
Sherpa Tharkey send me, Sahib.
He say: everything ready. I am porter, Sahib.
Then we shall have fun! . . . Good, tell Tharkey we are coming.
You're wondering what's going on? Well, you insisted on going, so I had another crack at Tharkey. I was luckier than you were the other day: I persuaded him to take us up there.
Captain, what can I say? You're a marvel!
Not so fast, not so fast! He's only agreed to take us as far as the wreck of the aircraft: no further. Still, once you're up there, at last you'll realise there isn't the remotest chance of finding anyone alive.
All the same, Tharkey has fixed up everything we need for the expedition: clothes, food, equipment and porters . . . But thundering typhoons, just my luck to be saddled with that fellow who behaves like a bull in a china shop!
An hour later . . .
Just think, here am I, fooling around at the back end of Nepal when I could be snoozing at Marlinspike, with a long, cool whisky at my elbow.
Whisky, by thunder! What about those bottles in my pack?
The grand old Duke of York ♩ ♫ He had ♪ ten thousand men . . . ♪ pom pom ♪ ♩ ♪

Great snakes! . . . He's off at full throttle! . . . Captain! . . . Hey, Captain, not so fast!
Well let him go . . . Road is long . . . Soon catch him up . . . You not worry!
. . . and he marched them down, hic, again
ZZZ . . . ZZZ . . . ZZZ
Hello, Professor, what are you doing here?
Lost my umbrella.
Your umbrella? Why, I've got a ship-load of them here . . . Heaven knows where they've come from.
Rubbish! This is a red pimento!
Check mate!
I . . . I don't know . . . I must have fallen asleep on my feet . . . The heat, I expect . . . I think I was dreaming . . .
That night . . .
Thundering typhoons, my poor feet. I expect they'll be better in the morning . . . Goodnight, everybody.
Goodnight, Sahib.
Goodnight, Captain.
Ah, my beauty past compare: these jewels bright I wear! . . .
!
?
!

Bianca Castafiore! . . . She's HERE, by thunder! That woman follows us to the ends of the earth!
Radio in porters' tent, Sahib.
Was I ever Margarita? Is it I?
He's right, by thunder! Well, I'll give them something to listen to!
Mind the guy ropes, Captain.
Thanks!
Come reply! Come reply! Tell me, Tell me truly!
Now then, you musical morons - just you pack up that confounded jukebox . . . and jump to it! Understand?
Thundering typhoons, can't a man get a moment's peace . . . anywhere?
ZZOINNG
?
Billions of blistering barnacles! It's about time they made a tent to stay up without all these fiddling bits of string!!
Next morning . . .
. . . with Haddock leading the rest of the field!
Oho! The river . . . across we go!
With my usual good fortune, this should end with a loud splash!
But this time I shan't give them the pleasure . . .
There! Just a few more yards, and I've made it!
Good heavens! The Captain!
SPLASH

Chucking stones in the river!... What a fright he gave us!
SPLASH
Yoohoo!
Look at me! Over already, without getting my feet wet either! How's that?
A remarkable performance, Captain! Congratulations! Just one thing: this isn't where we cross the river. Tharkey said the second bridge!
WHAT?
Billions of blistering barnacles!
Will he? Won't he?
Great snakes!
He will . . .
No . . . pity!
Well done, Captain. That's the safest way.
Not worth watching now . . .
Just a bark or two, and you can change my name to Snowy!
Later . . .
Golly, I could do with a drink.
That's lucky! A puddle of water.
Funny, that water tasted odd!
Wretched animal! What did you drink?
?

You unhappy creature! It was whisky! . . . Alcohol! Dragging an animal down to the level of man!
So what? Feels good, doesn't it? . . . Warms the cockles of your heart, eh?
What about some more?. . . Look-all that whisky, dripping away . . .
Ho! . . . Dog! Dog! . . . Look! . . . Look at dog!
?
Dog, him drunk! Ha! ha! ha!
!
?
Poor Snowy. He must be feeling the height.
Look out!
Look out!
What are those four all shouting about? . . . Something wrong?
SNOWY!

Great snakes! He'll be dashed to pieces on the rocks!
No, he's fallen in the water! What luck!
SPLASH
There, he's come up again!
To the bridge! It's our one chance of saving him!
If only I'm in time . . .
There! Now I've got him!
A little later . . .
Oh, there you are. So you managed to rescue the old drunkard?
Drunkard?
Yes! And you thought he had mountain sickness! Look: a broken whisky bottle in my rucksack . . . But it didn't all run to waste!
!
And what's more, if this ever happens again I shan't risk my neck saving you!
The long march goes on . . .
That is chorten, Sahib. Ashes of great lamas preserved there.
Stop, Sahib! Is bad luck!
Stop!
?
Ho!
?
Stop!

Well, what's up? Something the matter? What have I done?
It brings you bad luck, Sahib, if you pass right of a chorten.
Why? Am I breaking the Highway Code? Is this a one-way street?
Spirits are angry if man pass to right of chorten, Sahib. Then porters not dare to go on.
All right, all right, if it makes you happy.
Left or right, it's all the same to me, you know . . .
!?
Look out, Captain!
Stop, Captain! Stop! Stop!
Nothing I'd like better!
Keep to the left, Sahib!
Keep to the left! Keep to the left! I'd like to see you do it!
My whisky . . . safe . . . That's the main thing!
ZZING

The next morning . . .
You'd think we were in an Alpine forest.
Two hours later . . .
I wouldn't mind rhododendrons like these at Marlin- spike!
And that afternoon . . .
?
SPLOTCH
It's some sort of rotten fruit: it dropped from a tree.
I wonder which one it came from?
SPLOTCH
The following night . . .
We camp here, Sahib.
Look, we've reached the snow.
Across there, Tibet! Aeroplane wreck there. Tomorrow we arrive. Now, we eat. Tsampa is ready.
Tsampa? What's this stuff made of?
Tsampa, Sahib: cooked barley meal, with tea and butter.
HAW-HAWAAAW
What's that noise?
Yeti!
That . . . that . . . that is yeti!!
The yeti! The Abominable Snowman!!
WO-OW

The Abominable Snowman! That's a good one! Don't make me laugh! Fairy stories . . . old wives' tales! Who's ever seen this famous yeti?
Do not laugh, Sahib . . . Yeti is real. I not see him, but I know Sherpa Anseering . . . He see yeti . . . He much afraid . . . He run away.
And what was the yeti like?
Him very big, Sahib. Very strong. Him kill yaks with his fist . . . Yeti very bad. Eat eyes and hands of men he kill.
HAW-HAWAAAAW
?
!
Fiddle-faddle! You're imagining things . . . it's only the wind . . . But here's something real enough: a bottle of whisky!
Is that the sole survivor?
Ho! You not drink, Sahib!
Why ever not? Against your principles?
If yeti smell alcohol, he come . . . Yeti likes alcohol. One day near Sedoa he find chang, he drink it . . .
Drinking Chang? What on earth are you babbling about?
Chang, Sahib: is our drink. Very strong beer. Yeti take chang. Then get drunk, go to sleep. Men from village tie him up. But yeti very strong. When he no longer sleep . . .
He wakes up with a shocking hangover! I know!
Yes, Sahib: he wake up, break ropes, and there, off he goes!
You've made your point! . . . Well, I'm off to bed. Good night!
. . . And it'll take more than an abominable snowman to keep me awake, I can tell you!
?
YEOOOOW!
!

YEEOOOW!
My beard! It's caught in the zip!
One quick jerk, perhaps . . .
Got it!
EEK!
At daybreak . . .
I don't know, but . . . or . . . haven't I forgotten something?
Billions of blistering barnacles! . . . My bottle of whisky!
Now I remember; I must have left it where we had supper last night.
No! . . . But it WAS here . . .
GRRR
I say, Tintin. Did you pick up the bottle I left over there last night?
Me?
No. I thought you took it with you into your tent . . . What about Tharkey? . . .
Me? . . . No, Sahib. Other Sahib, perhaps? . . . Or porter?
No, Sahib.
No see it, Sahib.
Perhaps other Sahib? Or Sherpa Tharkey?
No, I tell you . . . Thundering typhoons, it can't have just vanished!
No, Sahib, alcohol not vanished . . .
Stolen, Sahib! Alcohol stolen by yeti!
Rubbish! What sort of village idiot d'you take me for? Half-baked Haddock?
Come, we start! . . . Long journey today.
No. No more start. We not go further.

Blistering barnacles, what's this? You won't go on? . . . What sort of pantomime is it this time?
We not go on, Sahib. We go home to our village.
We not want to be killed by yeti! . . . Him drink Sahib's alcohol; make him very bad now! . . .
I know, I know, the yeti walked off with my whisky . . . D'you think I'm soft in the head?
Thundering typhoons, not only do these Bashi-bazouks refuse to go on, they expect me to swallow their hocus-pocus into the bargain!
I speak with them . . .
The yeti drinking whisky! I expect he plays the bagpipes too!
Well? . . . Any luck? . . . My whisky?
They not know . . . But they go on. I say, they have chicken-hearts: when they come home all the village laugh at them . . . And then I tell them, Sahib is very generous . . . We go on.
Hey, Tintin! . . . What's up with that dog of yours? Look at him.
Snowy? Why?
Hey, Snowy! What's the matter?
GRRR
?
?
OH!
Look! Footmarks! . . . The Abominable Snowman!!
GRRR GRRRR

Tell me another! Have you fallen for that too? . . . Those footmarks were made by a bear. It's well known - bears do walk upright on their hind legs sometimes.
Anyway, we'll soon see . . . All we have to do is follow the tracks.
No, Sahib. You not do that! Be careful!
Be careful! . . . Be careful! . . . This yeti nonsense is beginning to get on my nerves!
Billions of bilious blue blistering barnacles! My bottle of whisky!
EMPTY!
RKRPXZKRMTFRZ!
My whisky, you Cro-Magnon! . . . My whisky, you Mameluke, you! . . . Vampire! . . . Dipsomaniac! . . . Body-snatcher!
You odd-toed ungulate! . . . Macrocephalic baboon! . . . Phylloxera! . . . Cannibal!
Diplodocus! . . . Filibuster! . . . Megalomaniac!
Come on, you old alcoholic, unless you're too scared!
Do not shout, Sahib . . . Avalanches!
Colocynth! . . . Troglodyte! . . . Pithecanthropus!

Kleptomaniac! . . .
Quick! . . . More snow may fall . . .
Ectoplasm!
OH! . . . Porters all gone!
!
!
YOOEE!
You come back, you poltroons!
poltroons . . .
troons
. . . oons
I wasn't addressing you up there!
That's not the yeti; it's the echo!
No answer . . . They see the footmarks of yeti; very frightened; they return home to village. Now we cannot go on.
Abandoning ship! . . . The lily-livered bandicoots!
?
But we simply must go on, Tharkey. We can't give up now, when we are so close to our goal.
Impossible, Sahib; we cannot carry porters' loads.
We'll each take an extra load; everything that isn't absolutely essential can be dumped here . . . Tharkey, we've got to save Chang! . . .

Next morning . . .
Nearly there . . .
Look . . . Aeroplane crash . . . down below.
Now you see . . . no one living here, Sahib.
Here, no . . .
Is it not true, Sahib? . . . Not possible to find anyone here . . . still alive.
It looks that way to me, and no mistake!
?
Look here!

It could have been Chang's . . . a present for his cousins . . .
Poor Chang! Why did you have to find that, of all things . . .
POOOOT
Careful, Sahib: avalanches!
Hello . . . Snowy seems to have found something to eat . . .
That's what he thinks!
Oh boy! This'll taste good!
GRRR
Poor old Snowy! You'll never manage it! . . . That chicken's frozen absolutely solid!
?
GRRR
GRRR
We camp here tonight, Sahib . . . Tomorrow return to the valley.
Well . . . I'm going to have a look around, over there, towards that rock-face . . .
. . . Because if I'd been in Chang's place, and I'd come out of the crash alive, that's where I would have headed . . .
I say, don't you think it's about time we had a breather?
. . . I'd have looked for a niche, or a cave, or a crack in the rock where I could shelter . . . But if that's what Chang did, why didn't he come out . . .
. . . when the rescue party arrived? . . . That's what puzzles me . . . Unless . . .
The mouth of a cave!
?
GRRR

Wait for a minute, while our eyes get accustomed to the dim light . . . Stop growling, Snowy.
GRRR
WUUUUW
!
No, it's only the wind getting up . . .
There's something carved on this flat rock . . . What does it say?
CHANG! . . . His name in Chinese! And he's carved it in our script too! . . .
TCHANG
So I wasn't mistaken! Chang did survive the accident . . . Chang sheltered here . . . But in heaven's name, what has become of him? Don't tell me he's here, quite close, in a dark corner of the cave!
CHANG!
CHANG!
BING
BANG
!
WOOAH!
Great snakes! When I shouted it made some bits of ice fall.
BING
WOOAH!
It's no use. We must come back with torches. I'd better hurry and join the others.
Heavens! It's snowing!
This is awful! You can't see ten feet ahead . . .
Two hours later . . .
Still nothing, Sahib!

This is crazy! I ought to have waited in the cave till it stopped. I've completely lost my bearings now.
COOEE!
No good! . . . Not a sound! The noise of the wind is drowning my voice. And it's getting dark, too. What'll become of us now, Snowy?
Only one thing to do . . . go on.
!
A crevasse! Crumbs, Snowy, that was a near thing!
!
We must be careful now. Keep close behind me Snowy, old boy.
Saved! . . . Someone's there! . . . Yes, look, it's the Captain!
GRRR
AHOY! CAPTAIN!
CAPTAIN! . . . HI! CAPTAIN!
He can't hear me! . . . This is awful! . . . CAPTAIN!
!
CAP . . .
?
Two hours pass by . . .
WOWOOOWOOOWOOW

It seems to be easing up a bit.
Sh! . . . Listen, Sahib!
WOWOOWOOW
Yeti!
Is he still around?
WOWOOWOOW
I advise him to keep his distance, the drunken old ape!
But that's no yeti . . . It's something else; I've heard that cry before . . . Let's go outside; we'll hear it better there.
WOWOOWOOW . . .
Listen!
Snowy! . . . It's Snowy, howling for the dead! Something must have happened to Tintin!
Tharkey, we must go and search for him at once!
I fetch ropes and torches, Sahib. We go immediately.
WOWOOW . . . WOWOW
There!
Snowy! . . . My poor Snowy! Where's your master? What's happened to your master?
WOW
Here, Sahib! . . . Fallen into crevasse!
Thundering typhoons!
TINTIN! TINTIN!

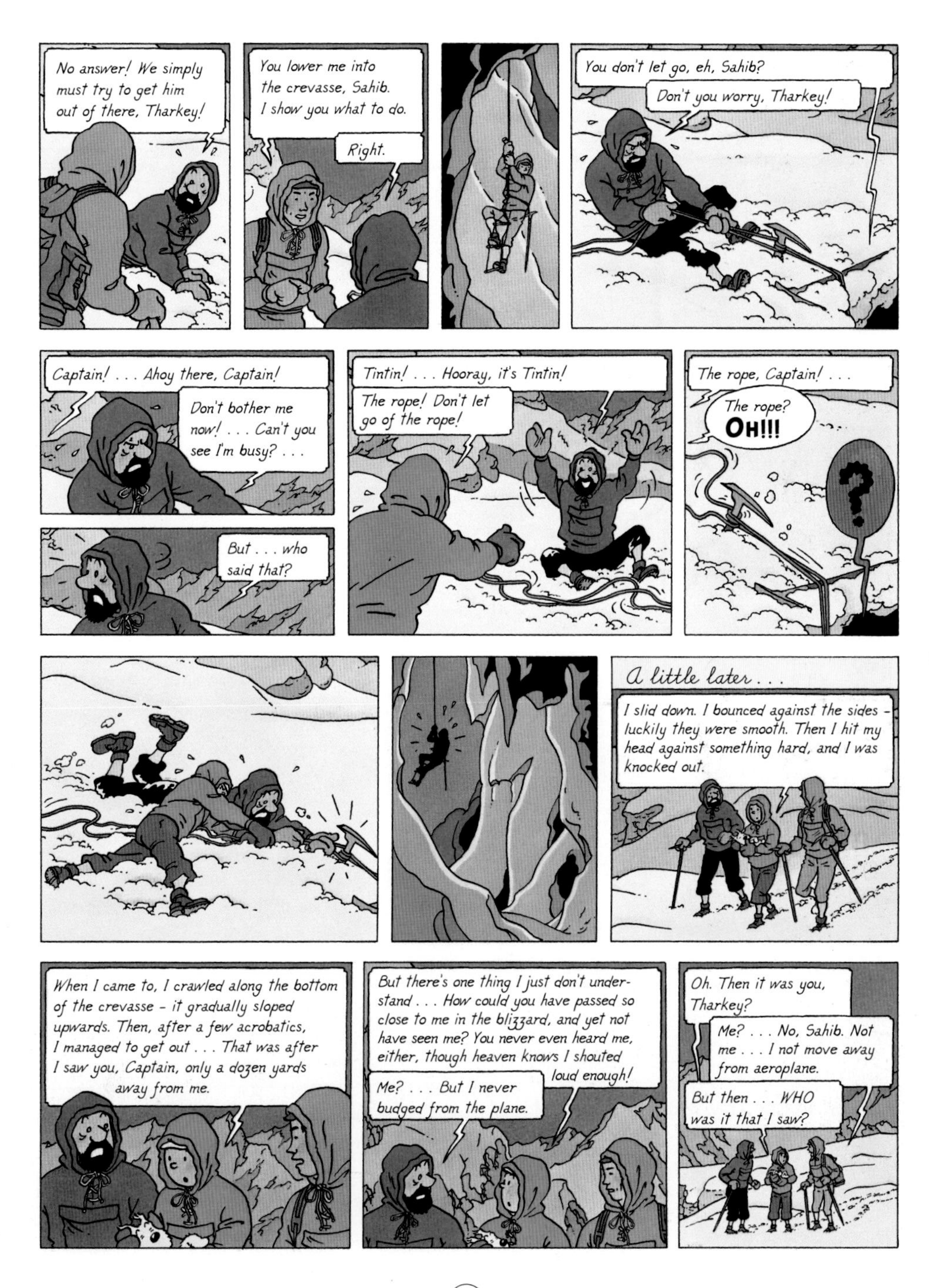
No answer! We simply must try to get him out of there, Tharkey!
You lower me into the crevasse, Sahib. I show you what to do.
Right.
You don't let go, eh, Sahib?
Don't you worry, Tharkey!
Captain! . . . Ahoy there, Captain!
Don't bother me now! . . . Can't you see I'm busy? . . .
But . . . who said that?
Tintin! . . . Hooray, it's Tintin!
The rope! Don't let go of the rope!
The rope, Captain! . . .
The rope? OH!!!
?
A little later . . .
I slid down. I bounced against the sides - luckily they were smooth. Then I hit my head against something hard, and I was knocked out.
When I came to, I crawled along the bottom of the crevasse - it gradually sloped upwards. Then, after a few acrobatics, I managed to get out . . . That was after I saw you, Captain, only a dozen yards away from me.
But there's one thing I just don't understand . . . How could you have passed so close to me in the blizzard, and yet not have seen me? You never even heard me, either, though heaven knows I shouted loud enough!
Me? . . . But I never budged from the plane.
Oh. Then it was you, Tharkey?
Me? . . . No, Sahib. Not me . . . I not move away from aeroplane.
But then . . . WHO was it that I saw?

You saw yeti, Sahib! . . . No doubt! . . . We go down quickly to valley. Great danger for us . . . Besides, no one alive up here . . .
But there is, Tharkey!
In an ice cave I discovered a stone on which Chang had carved his name . . . It absolutely proves that he survived the crash. I couldn't find anything more without a light. But as soon as we've taken care of Snowy, I suggest we all go and explore the cave.
Chang's name! . . . Then you were right after all!
At daybreak . . .
It was somewhere about there. But the snow last night has completely altered the landscape.
No, it wasn't as far as this . . . We must have passed the cave without noticing . . . Back again!
Look here, blistering barnacles, we've been going for two hours! Let's have a rest!
Later!
You can go on if you want to! I'm going to stop and sit down.
?
Here's your cave for you! When I start searching, I do the job properly!
Look: there's the stone I told you about.
But if Chang alive, Sahib, where is he now?
That's what I'm wondering, Tharkey.
I tell you, Sahib: your friend come here, yes . . . But afterwards, yeti kill him, and eat him up.
?
No Tharkey. In that case there'd be . . . it's too horrible . . . some traces of . . . of the tragedy.
!

Oh, Sahib! See!
!
No, thank heaven! It's the bone of an animal, like a chamois. But there should be others. Quick, let's look!
No, these are the bones of birds and small rodents.
Golly, this old yeti keeps a well-stocked larder!
But yeti perhaps eat Chang somewhere else . . . And how we find your friend under the snow?
I'm beginning to get a bit sick of this yeti business . . .
Ten thousand thundering typhoons, I wish he'd show up! Great flat-footed grizzly bear; I'd give him yeti!
We go back, Sahib. Nothing more to do here . . . Your friend dead, I am sure, Sahib.
Come on out, you big-head!
And Sahib, even if Chang alive . . .
. . . where can we search for him? . . . Where, Sahib? This way?
. . . Or that way?
I know, Tharkey. You're quite right: we must accept the evidence. Tomorrow we'll start making our way back to the valley.
The next morning . . .
Come on Tintin, old lad. You've done everything humanly possible . . . Come on now . . .
Goodbye, Chang! . . . Goodbye!

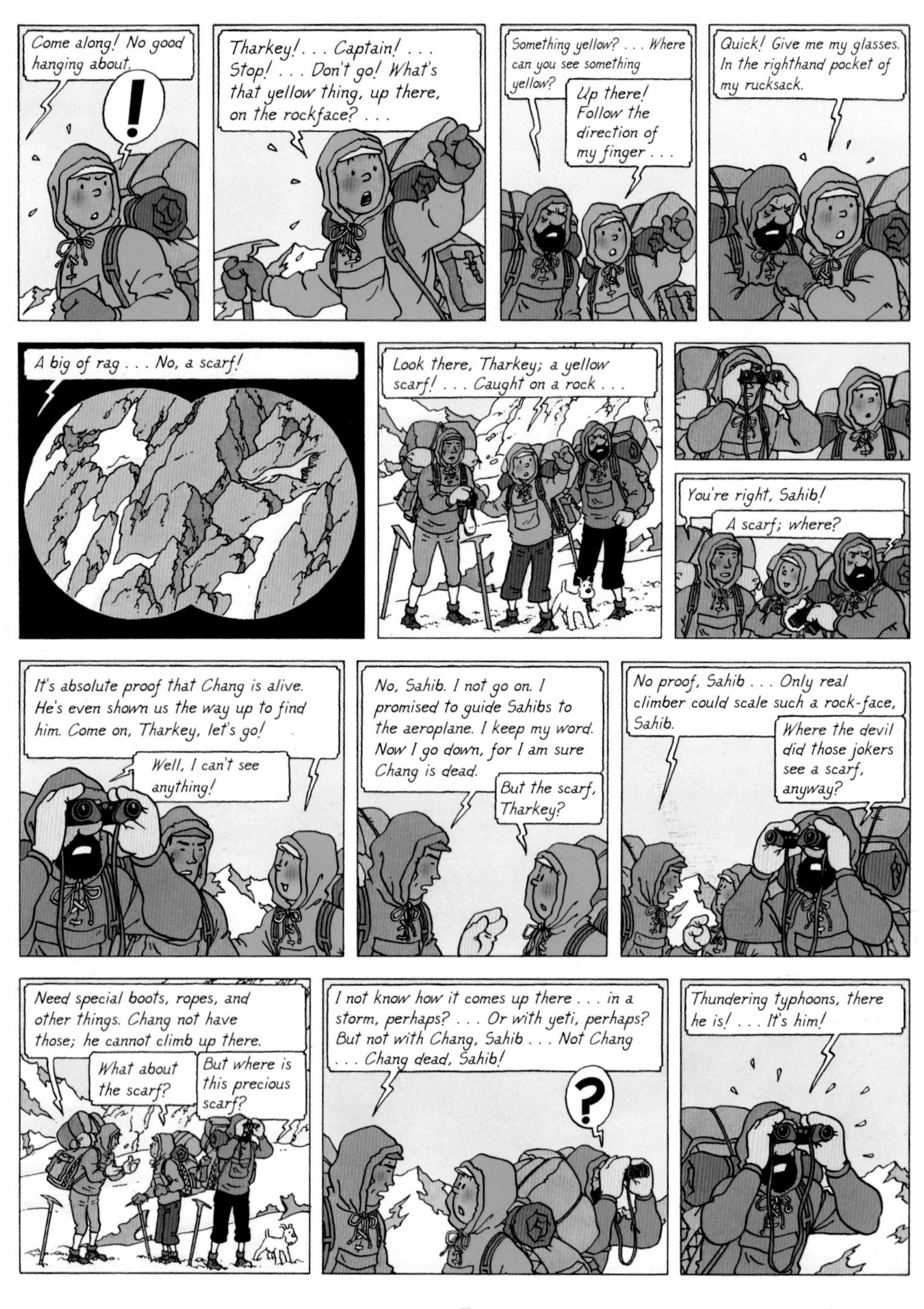

Come along! No good hanging about.
!
Tharkey! . . . Captain! . . . Stop! . . . Don't go! What's that yellow thing, up there, on the rockface? . . .
Something yellow? . . . Where can you see something yellow?
Up there! Follow the direction of my finger . . .
Quick! Give me my glasses. In the righthand pocket of my rucksack.
A big of rag . . . No, a scarf!
Look there, Tharkey; a yellow scarf! . . . Caught on a rock . . .
You're right, Sahib!
A scarf; where?
It's absolute proof that Chang is alive. He's even shown us the way up to find him. Come on, Tharkey, let's go!
Well, I can't see anything!
No, Sahib. I not go on. I promised to guide Sahibs to the aeroplane. I keep my word. Now I go down, for I am sure Chang is dead.
But the scarf, Tharkey?
No proof, Sahib . . . Only real climber could scale such a rock-face, Sahib.
Where the devil did those jokers see a scarf, anyway?
Need special boots, ropes, and other things. Chang not have those; he cannot climb up there.
What about the scarf?
But where is this precious scarf?
I not know how it comes up there . . . in a storm, perhaps? . . . Or with yeti, perhaps? But not with Chang, Sahib . . . Not Chang . . . Chang dead, Sahib!
?
Thundering typhoons, there he is! . . . It's him!

Blistering yetis, it's the barnacle! . . . I mean . . . Yettering barnacles, it's the blister . . . up there . . . I mean . . . the yeti!
I can't see it . . . Are you sure you . . . ?
Sure I'm sure! . . . A sort of enormous monkey . . . with a huge head like a coconut. He must have sensed that he'd been spotted; he bolted like a rabbit!
Well, yeti or no yeti, I'm going on. And you, Captain?
It's sheer lunacy, but I'll go with you. I've got a little score to settle with that pithecanthropic pickpocket up there!
And you, Tharkey . . . you?
No, Sahib, I not follow you. Very brave, Sahib, but you not know mountain dangers. Very foolish, Sahib . . .
Perhaps . . . Well, Tharkey, in that case this is where we part . . . But first we must settle up . . . The Captain will do it . . .
You do it, Tintin. I'm going to brew up.
Can you manage it, Captain?
Why not? It's as easy as pie. A child of three could do it. Perfectly simple . . .
Let's see . . . Five sevens are thirty-five; carry three. Five eights are forty: plus three, forty-three; carry four . . .
Don't forget the family allowances, and the national insur . . .
BOOM
WOW! OW!
A few minutes later . . .
Goodbye, Tharkey, and very many thanks. We couldn't have had a better guide.
Goodbye! . . . I hope you one day return to your own country!
Thanks, Tharkey . . . Goodbye!
Now, on our way . . . First objective: the yellow scarf!
Hey, Captain, what are you doing?

What am I doing? . . . Simple enough. I'm joining Tharkey. I'm going back with him.
But you agreed to go on . . .
Maybe, but now I've changed my mind . . . It's crazy to go ahead without a guide. I don't want to leave my bones in this benighted country!
Wait a minute.
Would you mind getting the flask in the back pocket of my rucksack? I'm terribly cold. A drop of brandy would set me right.
Did you say . . . er . . . brandy? You've still got some brandy?
Oh, it's only a little bottle I was keeping in reserve . . . Perhaps you'd like a drop too, Captain?
Would I? What a question!
GLUG
GLUG
Oh dear, it's empty already!
What about me?
Well, you know, alcohol is very bad for young people like you! . . . It's . . . it's deadly p-p-poison . . . Believe me, Tintin, there's n-n-nothing like t-t-total ab-ab-abstinence! Come along, now we-we-we'll rejoin Thar-Thar-Tharkey.
You know, Captain, on second thoughts, you're right to follow Tharkey. Better to give up . . . much wiser. The risk is far too great . . . In the first place, there's the yeti . . . It's just too bad if he thinks we've got cold feet . . .
WHAT?
C-c-cold f-feet? . . . Who has? . . . M-me? . . . S-s-scared of a ye-ye-yeti? . . . About turn, young fellow-me-lad . . . About t-t-turn! . . . Blistering barnacles, j-j-jump to it!
That did the trick!
Cold feet! . . . I'll sh-sh-show him, the scarecrow. I'll show him the sort of st-st-stuff Haddock's made of!
Not so fast!
C-c-cold feet! . . . ME!
Wait for me, Captain; we must rope up!
I suppose they think I've got wings!
Rope up yourself! . . . C-c-cold feet! Me! . . . Thundering ty-ty-typhoons! Let me tell you, when I-I-I meet your ye-ye-yeti the s-s-sparks will fly!
STOP!
E-E-E-EEK!
?

Tintin! . . . Tintin! . . . My ice-axe! What's happening?
It's nothing, Captain; just St. Elmo's fire. It's not dangerous. You're a sailor, surely you know it - an atmospheric phenomenon which sometimes makes flashes round the mast-head.
Thank goodness! I thought I'd turned into a sparking plug!
Wait for me this time; I'm coming.
First of all we're going to rope up. Then I'll jettison some of my load, so I can take Snowy up on my back.
Twenty minutes later . . .
We made it! . . . Here's the scarf!
Oh, Captain! Look at it! Bloodstains!
Yes, I can see . . . But even supposing that this is Chang's scarf, what then? . . . What do you suggest we do now, eh?
Go on, Captain . . . Chang came this way. We must follow this pathway to the top.
You call this a pathway!? . . . Oh, all right.
Careful, Captain. This is rather tricky.
To think there are people who do this for fun!
!

YOW!!
Blistering barnacles! That was a near thing . . . But I'm safe, thanks to you . . . and the rope. Amazing stuff, nylon! . . . Now, can you haul me up towards you? . . .
No such luck! If I make the slightest move, it's the high dive for us both!
Blistering barnacles! What are we going to do now?
And, thundering typhoons, there's no way of regaining a foothold on that perishing rockface.
It's hopeless . . . I can't make it! And I'm beginning to freeze on the end of this bit of string . . . Can you hang on up there?
For as long as possible . . . But I can feel myself getting weaker, and paralysed with cold.
Poor Captain. He obviously doesn't realise - with each jerk the rope cuts further into me.
Which means we both fall! That's no good, young fellow. You, at least, can save yourself. You must cut the rope: it's the only answer!
Never! Either we're both saved, or we die together! . . .
You're talking nonsense! Better for one to die, rather than two, isn't it? . . . Cut the rope, Tintin!
Never, you hear me? . . . I'll never do that!
All right, I'll do it myself . . . Get my knife . . . and that's it . . . Cast off moorings!
Thundering typhoons! . . . I can't get the confounded blade open! My fingers are completely numb . . . Ah, that's it! . . .

Captain, I implore you! Don't do it! You're mad!
No! Blistering barnacles! My mind is made up!
Oh! Clumsy fool!
?!
YOOO-E-E
YOOO-E-E
?
YOOO-E-E
It's Tharkey's voice! . . . Tharkey! . . . We're saved!
A few moments later . . .
But tell us, Tharkey; what were you doing - to find us here?
I go towards my village, but I think of you . . . You, young white sahib risking your life to save Chinese friend . . . Me yellow man, like him, but I not want to help . . . I tell myself I am coward. I turn back, and follow you . . .
Good for you, Tharkey! . . . Shall we go on together now?
That night . . .
Pitch camp quick behind rocks; storm comes!
Hold tight! I bring stones to fix tent!
Hurry, Tharkey!
HELP! The tent! . . .
Blistering barnacles! Let go! . . . Let go!

The tent's gone! . . .
Blown away! . . .
Lost in the night!
Ssh! . . .
You listen!
HAW-HAW-HAW
Yeti!!
What's that jackass doing out of doors at this hour?
HAW-HAW-HAW! . . .
HAW-HAW-HAW-HAW
THUMP
?
?
HOUI! HOUI! HOUI! HOUI! HOUI!
What's happened? He must have hurt himself.
Serves him right!
Houi . . . Houi . . . Houi . . .
We pitch my little tent for tonight. It is only tent for one. Very difficult for three to come in . . .
We'll never all get inside this!
Well, we've got to!
Try to squeeze up a bit more, Captain!
A fat lot of use that is! . . . We're already packed like sar . . . aaar . . . aaaaaar . . .
AAAAAARTCH . . .
No, Captain, no! You musn't! . . .
TCHOOO

That is big, big disaster! If now we stay here, we freeze. We must move . . .
We go down now fast as possible . . . We cannot spend more time seeking Chang.
Oh, Chang!
Two days later . . .
This is it: I've had enough. For three days we've been on the go, without sleep. I'm done: I'm not moving another step.
Come on, Captain, just one last effort. In a few hours we'll be below the snowline.
No. Go on without me.
I've still got a little brandy left. Here, come on, have a drop.
I don't care. Even if you fill me up with jet fuel, I won't budge another inch!
Tintin Sahib! . . . Tintin Sahib! . . . Look!
A monastery! . . . We're saved!
There we can sleep, Sahib!
Get up, Captain! A monastery!
It'd take more than an earthquake to shift me!
CRACK
Look out! We not stop here!
CRACK
?
?

BROOMMM
BROOMM
The White Goddess is angry! It is a portent.
Really, Blessed Lightning, you're as gullible as a Poh-Pryang peasant! It's an avalanche; neither more nor less.
!?
Look, Blessed Lightning ascends into the air. He is going to have another vision!
Blessed Lightning and his visions! . . . When you think, he's as blind as a bat from Wei-Pyiong!
Silence, Shining Light! Blessed Lightning speaks!
I see three men . . . no, two men and a young boy with a great heart . . . And a little dog, white as powder snow . . . They are in mortal danger . . .
Great Heart is walking . . . walking . . . walking . . . He is at the end of his strength . . . Great Heart falls . . .
YEOW! . . .
WOWOOWOOW
!
MMMH . . .

What a terrible monster! . . . It's going to eat Tintin!
?
EEK!
Wooah! Wooah!
A yak! It nearly strangled me!
I must save the others! I must reach that monastery, at all costs . . .
No, it's hopeless. With this twisted ankle I can't go on . . . Oh, what can I do? . . . What can I do?
Snowy! It's up to you to save us now, Snowy . . . You must carry this message and get help from the monastery . . .
Go, Snowy, go! . . . Our lives depend upon you! Go on, quickly!
This message! . . . Carry this message . . . Carry this message . . . Carry . . .
?
Golly, what a magnificent bone! . . . It's certainly a five-star model! . . . What a bone!
Stay, Snowy! . . . Your duty! . . . The message!
Stuff and nonsense! The message will keep! But you don't see a bone like that every day!
S.O.S! HELP!

The message!?!
Vanished!
What will Tintin say?!?
There's only one thing I can do . . .
To the monastery, double quick! Message or no message, I'll make them follow me.
Half an hour later . . .
Here comes the young Lobsang, back from his walk.
Where has that dog come from? . . . I've never seen him round here before.
Wooah! Wooah!
What does he want with me? . . . Stop it, you horrid animal!
Come with me! We must save Tintin!
By the White Goddess! . . . A mad dog! . . . Help!
Come with me, boy!
Help! . . . Help! . . . Heelp!
A mad dog! Help! Help! . . .
Help! . . .
Wooah! Wooah!
We must trap the brute in a corner!
He's cornered! . . . Careful, now; don't miss him!
Wooah! Grr! Grr! Wooah!

Stop! Do not touch that dog!
?
?
It is undoubtedly Powder Snow, the dog that Blessed Lightning saw in a vision, only a little while ago.
There must be men in danger on the slopes of the White Goddess! We must go and look for them!
You see, we have only to follow him; he shows us the way.
Two days later . . .
DONG
DONG DONG DONG
All right! All right! I'm coming!
Come on! Show a leg there! Time we were on our way!
!?
Blistering barnacles, you're a handsome pair!
Obviously we must be in a monastery . . .
But how the devil did we end up here?

It's a kite!
Boy monks, flying kites . . . Not a very serious occupation, I must say!
They're quite happy . . . while no one seems to be bothering about me! I'd better spy out the land . . . First of all, where are my boots?
Hey, what the . . . ?! Either my feet have swollen, or my boots have shrunk . . . They simply won't . . .
CRACK
!
Thundering typhoons! That's a good start!
Meanwhile . . .
Welcome, O Travellers, to the monastery of Khor-Biyong . . . But I thought there were three of you?
They say our friend is still asleep, Grand Abbot . . . He was completely exhausted.
Yes, it seems that you men from other lands have a strange, uncontrollable desire to climb the highest mountains at all costs, even at the risk of your lives. Why is this?
In our case, Grand Abbot, it is not a search for glory, nor a love of climbing that brings us here. Our aim was . . .
RAT
TAT
TAT
?
Er . . . I beg your pardon, but . . . has anyone got a shoe-horn?

Tintin! . . . Tharkey! . . . How wonderful to see you!
Welcome to you also, noble stranger. Please be seated.
Thanks . . . er . . . Grand Admiral.
Pray continue, young stranger; you were speaking of the real purpose of your journey.
Well, Grand Abbot, it's like this: there was an air disaster recently, in Nepal, in which all the passengers were said to have perished. A friend of mine, a young Chinese named Chang, was in that plane.
Yes, er . . . Grand Vizier. And just because he saw Chang alive in a dream, this young whippersnapper got a bee in his bonnet: about rescuing him. And because he's as stubborn as a mule, he rushed off to Nepal. And I, like the old fool that I am, came trailing after him.
We tramped for days and days and days! . . . We hauled ourselves up vertical rock-faces! We baked in the sun and froze in the snow! We tumbled down into bottomless crevasses! We were walloped on the head by avalanches! Worst of all, er . . . Grand Mufti, the yeti pinched a bottle of whisky! Only just opened: and the last one I had left!
And to crown everything, er . . . Grand Turk, there was as much sign of Chang as there's hair on his head!
What did he say? What is there on my head?
So . . . for the sole purpose of searching for your friend Chang you braved all these dangers, and you would have died had your dog not warned us? . . .
Well . . . yes, Grand Abbot.
Alas, young stranger, here in Tibet the mountains keep those whom they take. And the vultures make sure that no traces remain. Such will have been the fate of your friend Chang. You will never, never find the slightest sign of him.
There's one, anyway!
?
!
?

And the other one's going to follow suit, or I'll know the reason why!
Yes, brave young man, you must abandon all hope; never again will you see the friend so dear to your heart . . .
Your wisest course is to return to your own country . . . Moreover, the rule of our order forbids us to harbour strangers. Tomorrow a caravan leaves here, bound for Nepal. May I invite you to join it?
That's a good idea, er . . . Grand Panjandrum.
The next morning . . .
The caravan is ready to leave, noble travellers.
Thank you, Reverend Father. We're quite ready. We'll follow you.
So, we're on our way home . . .
Without Chang, alas!
Yes, without Chang . . . but what could you expect? It was hopeless from the start, Tintin. I always said so.
Great Heart, you have forgotten this!
Why, it's Chang's scarf.
It's really very kind of you . . .
!?!¿
I see . . . I see . . . the horn of the yak. Below, the eye . . . a cave . . . I see . . . I see a boy . . . this scarf belong to him . . . He is lying on a couch of juniper branches . . .
Impossible! There must be a catch in it!
Alas! He is possessed by devils . . . He has a fever . . But who is this approaching him? I cannot see clearly . . Ah, now I see better . . . it . . .
A photo, quick; no one will ever believe us.
OOOOH! THE MIGOU!

Pity! Too late to snap the flying father! He's come down to earth!
Quick, tell me, where is Chang?
Where is who?
Chang! Chang! . . . The boy you saw lying on the juniper branches . . . Where is he?
I do not understand what you mean . . . Please, you left this scarf . . . Go in peace, young traveller.
But . . .
He saw Chang! Obviously ill, but alive! I'm sure of it!
?
Tintin, for heaven's sake! Surely to goodness you don't believe in that flying saucer? He was talking a lot of mumbo-jumbo!
I'm certain it was real!
Come on! We must see the Grand Abbot.
Must have a screw loose!
The Horn of the Yak . . . There is a mountain of that name, three days' march from here, near the village of Charahbang. What more did he say?
He mentioned an eye, and a cave.
Billions of blistering barnacles, don't tell me you're taking all this hocus-pocus seriously!
You must know, noble stranger, that many things occur here in Tibet which seem unbelievable to you men of the West.
Then he described my friend Chang, lying on a bed of branches. He saw someone approaching Chang, and then, as though terrified, he shouted: "The migou!" . . . What did he mean by the migou? . . .
The migou?. . . You are sure you heard aright: the migou? It is the name given here to the Abominable Snowman. In Nepal they call it the yeh-teh, or yeti; here it is the migou.
But then . . . Grand Abbot?
Do not enter. He is speaking with the strangers.
Then it would be better if your friend were dead, for he is a prisoner of the migou. And the migou never surrenders his prey!
!
?

Chang a prisoner of the Abominable Snowman!! . . . But that's dreadful! . . . We simply must save him, Grand Abbot!
Alas, it is impossible, Great Heart. No one would run such a risk.
Very well, I'll go alone if necessary. My friend is in danger. You can't expect me to desert him now.
No! You shan't go! Neither alone, thundering typhoons, nor with me! You got round me once, but it won't happen again! . . . There's been enough skylarking! I won't have any more! You'll come home to Marlin-spike with me, blistering barnacles, and there's an end to it!
Just where is this mountain they call the Horn of the Yak?
Say something to him, Grand . . . Grand . . . Grand Father! . . . Make him give up this crazy idea!
Near the village of Charahbang, three days' march from here . . . There, only a few days ago, a yak was killed by the migou.
There, you see!
Listen, Captain, don't be angry with me . . . I'm leaving tomorrow for Charahbang. You go with Tharkey and rejoin the caravan . . . You must understand: I can't do otherwise.
All right, you do as you please! Go as far as you like and look for this Chang of yours! You can go to Mars for all I care! I'm packing my bags and going home . . .
. . . before someone gets hurt!
Charahbang – three days later.
A stranger! A stranger!
Hello! . . . Hello! . . . Could you take me to the village headman?
You come! You come!
Guide? . . . To go to Horn of Yak? . . . No one, Koucho, no one! . . . Horn of the Yak . . . Migou! . . . Migou!
?
There!
Look!
Another one!

You little scallywags! . . . Is that what they teach you in school, eh? . . .
Impossible! I must be dreaming!
Same to you, cheeky!
!
Captain! . . . You, here!!!
Yes . . . and would you believe it: this bunch of young scamps – they had the nerve to put out their tongues at me!
But of course, Captain: that's how you greet people in Tibet . . . Now, tell me what you're doing here . . . I thought . . .
Oh . . . you . . . you're surprised, eh? . . . Well, you see . . .
Er . . . I . . . you . . . I'd kept the camera . . . so I thought . . . I said to myself: I'll take it to him. The Grand Piano lent me horses, and a guide . . .
How kind of him . . . And you're going straight back?
Er . . . you know, since I'm here I think I may as well go a little of the way with you . . .
Oh, that'd be wonderful . . . But I haven't found anyone yet to take me . . . to take us to the Horn of the Yak.
Horn of the Yak?! . . . Not go there, Koucho! Not go! . . . Migou up there; migou! . . . Last week him kill yak, just near village!
Where abouts? Could you show me?
An hour later . . .
Here, Koucho . . . Here shepherd found yak dead, killed by migou.
This is it! Look, Captain! We don't need a guide: Snowy will show us the way. He's picked up the scent already.
You've been very kind, bringing us this far . . . Run back home now . . . Goodbye, my friend. And thank you.
You not go! . . . Migou kill you!
Goodbye . . . Tibetan style! . . . NNH!
Off we go, on the last lap! . . .
Yah!

?
GNAAAAH!
Hey Captain, What's up? Are you coming?
Yes, I'm coming ...
. . . but that young monkey needed a lesson in good manners!
The next morning . . .
What a hope! You're just going to stumble on the den of this teddy-bear, I suppose? It'd be a miracle!
It would if we had nothing to go on . . . But thanks to Snowy, we're on the right track . . . Now then, our next objective is a mountain that looks like a yak's horn.
Easy to talk!
There! . . . What did I tell you? . . . See . . . it's unmistakable: that mountain there. Look at the shape!
We must try to arrive at the foot of the mountain at nightfall, and make sure our tent is well hidden.
Three days later . . .
Look here, Tintin, I'm getting fed up! Here we've been for three days, waiting for this confounded migou of yours to poke his nose out . . . Besides . . .
The monk, Blessed Lightning, said the eye. You remember, Captain: the eye below the horn. We must keep watching the eye . . . Patience, Captain, patience!
Patience! . . . For all we know, we might sit here waiting for seven years! . . . If I could even have a good smoke . . . But no. Poor delicate little fellow . . . his nose is so sensitive! I don't mind telling you . . .
HAWAAAW!
!
?

The yeti! I can see it! It's just come out from behind a rock, over there!
It's going . . . It's disappeared. This is it - now's our chance. Come on, Captain! Not a moment to lose!
What can we do?
Go straight to his den - to rescue Chang! Come on! . . . Hurry!
You . . . I . . . don't forget the camera . . .
Think! . . . If you could get a photograph of the yeti, imagine what a sensation it would cause!
I'll try.
Stop!
You stay here and keep a look-out. If you see him coming back, give a whistle!
OK . . . Remember the photograph!
!
The entrance to the cave!
I should never have let him go alone . . . I only hope nothing goes wrong . . .

Chang! . . . Chang! . . .
Who . . . Who's there? . . . Who is it?
Chang! . . . Chang! . . . It's me! . . . It's Tintin!
Chang! . . . My poor Chang! . . .
Tintin!
I knew I'd find you in the end! . . . This is wonderful!
Tintin! Oh, how often I've thought of you!
But you're ill; you're shaking with fever . . . Come, we must hurry. Wrap yourself up in my anorak and we'll go.
No, Tintin, I can't!
I haven't the strength to move . . . Besides, supposing he comes back.
There's no danger. One of my friends is waiting outside. Any sign of the yeti, and he'll whistle . . .
He . . . Why didn't I hear him coming? . . . Qu-qu-quick . . . I must whistle . . .
FFFH
PPPH
ZZZ
WWH
Lean on me - hold tight. You'll see, we'll manage.
TINT . . . BGLLB . . . TINTIN! LOOK OU-U-U-U-T!

GRHAWAARH
Help! Fire! Murder! Whatever shall I do?
HAWAARRH!
Action stations! Full steam ahead! Charge!
HWAAARRH!
!?
Hang on, Tintin! . . . Here I come! . . .

Captain! . . . Captain! . . . Heavens! Are you hurt?
An atom bomb! An atom bomb!
What happened? . . . An atom bomb, wasn't it? . . . Are we all dead?
No, it was the yeti. Here, get up.
Quick! Chang's there! We must carry him to the camp at once. The yeti was blinded by the flash-bulb, but he may come back.
Two hours later . . .
Well, I'd better tell you the whole of my story . . .
VT-DRO
AIR INDIA
DRO
I caught the plane from Patna to Katmandu. It was glorious weather, and everyone on board was very cheerful. But, shortly before we were due to arrive, we ran into a violent storm.
The aircraft was tossed all over the place, and although the crew did their best to reassure us, we feared the worst. Then suddenly there was a terrible crash . . . and I blacked out . . .
When I came to I was lying in the snow. My legs hurt dreadfully. Wreckage of every description was littered all around me . . .
Except for the wind, there wasn't a sound; not a shout, nothing . . . I was the sole survivor of that horrible disaster!
Panic-stricken, I struggled to my feet. I didn't feel the pain; I had only one thought: to get away. At last, at the end of my strength, I found a niche in the rock. There, I fainted again . . .
How long I remained unconscious I don't know. But when I came round, I almost died of fright . . .
In the half-light of a cave, an enormous head was looming over me, and two gleaming eyes were staring at me . . .
HAW-HAWAOUOUH!

HAWAAOUOUH!
What a heart-rending cry! You'd think he was in distress.
It's not very surprising . . . He seemed to become quite fond of me. At first he brought me biscuits he found in the wreckage of the plane. Later I lived on plants and roots he brought back from his nightly prowls.
Sometimes he brought me little animals. It was revolting, but I forced myself to eat them . . . Little by little I regained my strength, until I could stand. Then I had the idea of carving my name on a rock.
Yes, we found the cave, Chang, and saw the stone with your name on it. Then, later, we found your scarf.
Oh, yes, my scarf. I'll tell you about that . . .
One morning, the yeti came rushing back. He seemed very frightened. He picked me up, and ran off with me in his arms . . .
Then began that dizzy climb up a sheer cliff!
I was terrified . . . But he was amazingly sure-footed. Holding on with only one hand, he leaped from rock to rock like a chamois . . . He stopped for a moment, then I saw what was happening.
Far away, a column of men was heading for the wrecked aircraft . . . And the yeti was carrying me away from them!
I screamed and yelled to attract their attention. But my voice was too weak. Then I undid my scarf and threw it over the edge, hoping someone would see it and follow our tracks.
That's just what we did, Chang . . . But what then?
The yeti carried me on. Another storm blew up. I was frozen. I don't know how long that fantastic journey lasted – I was only half-conscious . . . All I know is . . .
. . . I ended up in the cave where you found me, shaking with fever and exhaustion . . . I was utterly dejected: no one would find me.
I would die there, alone, miserably, far from my family and friends.

Blistering barnacles, I've had enough! I can't bear any more . . . you'll have to wait while I get my handkerchief.
POOOT
HAWAAAAAAAAH!
?
!
?
HAWAAAAAAAAAH!
So there you are, you ante-diluvian bulldozer! . . . Come closer, if you dare, you jobbernowl, and I'll turn you into a hearth-rug!
Poor Snowman, what a fright he got. The Captain scared him away when he blew his nose!
MEGACYCLE! PYROMANIAC!
You said "Poor Snowman" . . . How strange. The only one who knows him, and you don't call him "abominable".
Of course I don't, Tintin: he took care of me. Without him I'd have died of cold and hunger.
A few days later . . .
The strangers!
The strangers come back!
Yes, here we are, back again . . . and the migou hasn't eaten us! . . . We need porters, to carry this boy to the monastery.
Three days later . . .
We're nearly there, Chang. You'll soon be on the mend.
Pack up your troubles in your old kitbag and pom pom pom?
POM
TOOOT
ZZING
DONG
BOOM
TINGALING
?

The Grand Abbot! It must be something very special, to bring him out in full procession! . . .
Greetings, O Great Heart . . . Following our custom, I present you with this scarf of silk. Blessed Lightning told us of your approach, and I have come to meet you, so that I may bow in deference before you.
Before me, Grand Abbot? . . . But . . .
Yes, what you have achieved, few would have dared to undertake. Blessings upon you, Great Heart, for the strength of your friendship, for your courage, and for your steadfastness.
You too, Rumbling Thunder – blessings upon you, for in spite of all, you have the faith that moves mountains.
Moves them? I'd sooner flatten them!
And here is the boy whom you snatched from the jaws of the migou. Blessings upon you, young man, for you inspired great devotion in the hearts of these two strangers.
What about me? Don't I get a word?
Is that thing a trumpet? I suppose you blow in here . . .
POOOAA
Oh, sorry!

A week has passed . . .

How are you feeling now, Chang?
Much better! . . . A good rest, and being so well looked after - I've completely recovered.

Fine! And thanks to those kind monks who organised this caravan for us, we'll soon be back in Nepal - and then on our way to Europe.
HAWAAAOUH!
!
!
That old reprobate again!

A goodbye from the yeti, Chang . . . Now he's alone again . . . until someone from an expedition manages to catch him.
A present from Tibet!

You know, I hope they never succeed in finding him. They'd treat him like some wild animal. I tell you, Tintin, from the way he took care of me, I couldn't help wondering if, deep down, he hadn't a human soul.
Who knows?

The
END